QUEST
for the First Hive

Verity Jenkins

Quest for the First Hive

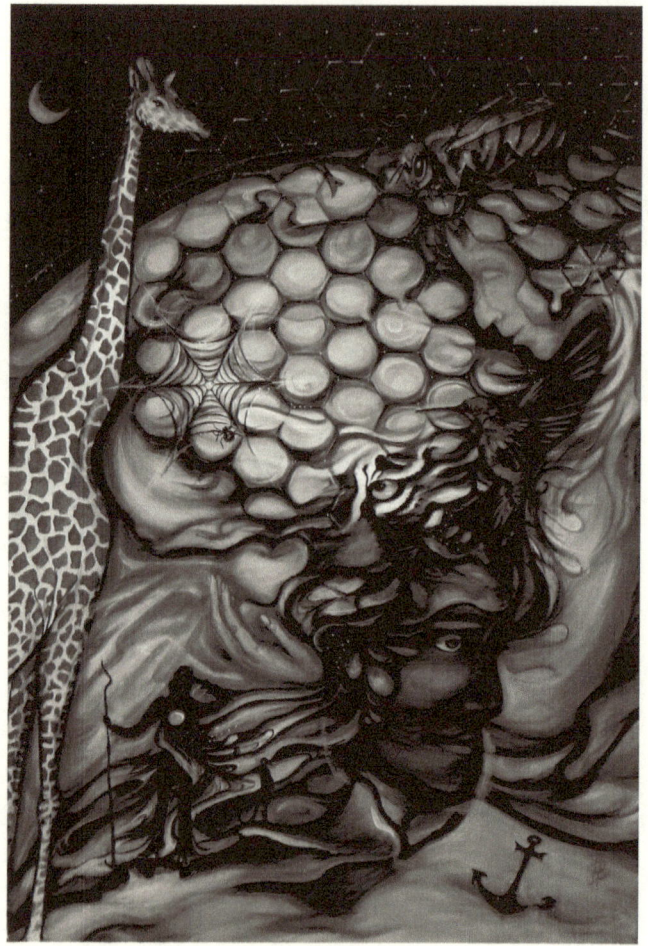

Artwork by Biljana Banchotova

ISBN: 978-0-9936492-5-7

FORWARD

This is the first story in what has become The Ray Adventure Series. Writing *Quest for the First Hive* was easy, it came from a place of inspiration; a five year old opened up her hand and told me she was going to love a very dried bee back to life. That message of loving something back to life touched me so deeply. There are times when we all need to be loved back to life - and love others back to life.

Because of this inspiration the story literally wrote itself during the most creatively effortless month of my life.

Ray is more than a character in a story - more than a twelve-year-old girl - Ray is you and me. I have written this story as a love letter to the adventurous, storytelling, world-changing trickster in you.

This is a story for all ages - twelve to one-hundred and twelve.

Hope you enjoy,

Verity Jenkins
Whitestone Ontario
Dec 2022

COPYRIGHT

ACKNOWLEDGEMENTS

I owe a debt of gratitude for the work of Laurens van der Post for his insights and understanding of the !Kung - one of the San peoples who have traditional been nomadic and lived throughout the Kalahari desert and have now been settled to the Western edge (formerly known as the Bushman of the Kalahari). The insights I gained from the extraordinary books, Lost World of the Kalahari, and Heart of the Hunter have much influenced Quest for the First Hive - especially the character of uLangalibalela the Witch Doctor. I would highly recommend any of Lauren van der Post's books, but my favourites are Lost World of the Kalahari, Heart of the Hunter and Jung: the Story of our Time.

I have not used the older term: Bushmen of the Kalahari, as was the practice in Laurens van der Post's time but the more contemporary term of !Kung San.

www.verityjenkins.com

Verity Jenkins

QUEST FOR THE FIRST HIVE

Book 1

Quest for the First Hive

Verity Jenkins

CHAPTER ONE
ANTICS AT THE TORONTO ZOO

Ray and Fa

"You are my drop of golden sunshine," he'd say to her just as he turned out the light. They were a pair of storytellers. Even when Fa was away travelling, they wrote stores and sent them to each other. Bedtime storytelling usually involved their both telling parts of a story together, and somehow their favourite animal, the giraffe, would sneak in.

"Goodnight, Fa," she'd say.

"Goodnight, Ray," he'd say, and then pretty soon she'd be in a world that was not too far from the stories they shared.

One day, Fa was not there for storytime; he had gone off to a faraway land where Ray could not reach him.

***

One morning, Mum looked particularly sad, and although I was sad, too, I decided to think of ways to cheer Mum up.

"Let's go and see a giraffe," I suggested to Mum.

She thought it was a good idea, too, and so off we headed to the zoo that was nestled in the lush, green Rouge Valley. We caught the small train that ran through the zoo, passing the chimpanzees that I liked because they were not very well behaved and were frequently arguing and throwing coconuts at each other. Then past the elephant that was sulking in the corner because he had been unfairly told off for watering a Grade 2 class that, to the elephant, and to my mind, obviously needed cooling down. Then, still some way off, we both caught sight of the giraffe, whose head rose up through the crown of trees, even though he was not yet fully grown.

Giraffes and their Special Powers

I know a quite a lot about giraffes because Fa and I would visit them and talk with the zookeeper. And Fa'd been to Africa and seen them in the wild. The giraffe's eyesight and long view are their main defence from tigers and other predators. In the past, most zookeepers thought that other than the few sounds baby giraffes make, older giraffes become silent and lose their vocal cords. This is a myth. Their vocal cords do atrophy (which is a fancy way of saying "dry out"), but they atrophy because they gain a more advanced way to communicate, a way of communicating great distances without anyone else hearing them. Scientists have only recently discovered how: They call it infrasonics, which are very low-frequency sound waves--so low that humans can't hear them. The only other animals that have this ability that we know of are whales, rhinoceroses, and elephants, none of which are the giraffe's predators and most of which are herbivores like the giraffe.

I'm a herbivore, too; or for some reason we're called vegetarians. Well, I'm not a strict vegetarian. I decided not to eat anything that loves because I know what it's like to have lost someone you love. So I guess I'm a loveatarian. And I'm not yet convinced that fish love, especially the smaller ones, like anchovies and krill. So you could say that I eat like a whale, mostly plants and some smaller fish like sardines.

On a bit of a flaky website, it said that there are a few people who are attuned to ultra-low frequencies and can feel these sound waves. Maybe if I were more like the giraffe, I could hear what it was saying. This is what I very much wanted to be able to do.

In fact, according to Fa, these hidden powers give the giraffe the ability to listen to dreams and thoughts and to see what is to come. "What do you think those two little bumps on top of the giraffe's head are really for?" Fa would say on most of our visits to the zoo. Well, those two little bumps, sometimes three, which look like stunted antlers, are to protect the giraffe's head, but it does make sense that they could also do something else. Some other girls thought this was silly and didn't matter, but I have discovered that this world is really a very silly place, and the sillier it is, the more likely that it's true.

It was just like one of Fa's favourite sayings, "When it's nighttime in Paris, it's Wednesday over here."

"Now that's just plain silly," I'd say to Fa.

"Silly but true," Fa would say.

The King of Kings and the Queen of Queens

This was one story I asked Fa to tell over and over again. Once upon a time, in a land that is awake when we are fast asleep . . . in a place where time moves more slowly than it does here . . . where the Great Eastern Sun is larger and the people smaller. In a place where the great grey, green, greasy Limpopo River flows like a giant snake though jungles and past villages with names like Timbuktu. In the midst of this is the most wondrous place of all, The Great Kalahari Desert. A place where animals as large as dinosaurs roam wild to this day, and the first humans still walk the earth. In this place lived a King; not just any King, but a King of Kings whom every living thing both loved and served, as he loved and served them. He was the greatest of all giraffes. The other giraffes would travel great distances and listen to the thoughts of all of the people, animals, and living things and would report back to the King of Kings. (I guess they would need to summarize a fair bit like my teacher keeps telling me to do.) This way, the King ruled and served all living things.

In this land, there was also a Queen of Queens. As the King was the tallest of all of the animals, the Queen of Queens ruled the smallest. She commanded a vast army of drones that kept the hives safe and ensured that everyone got what they wanted most: honey. The land flowed with Milk and Honey. It was a time of great peace, happiness, and abundance for all. The King of Kings saw what was happening throughout his kingdom and was the greatest of all listeners; and the Queen of Queens made sure that all the crops were pollinated, and there was honey enough for all.

"Sweet," I would say.

"What more could anyone want?" said Fa.

Then one day, the tigers, leopards, and lions began to attack the giraffes and killed the King. They ruined the great hives, kept the honey to themselves, and brought fear into the world. Only a few were able not to fall prey to fear: these were the Rays, her father said. In dark times, when people live in either Fear or Greed, the Rays are needed most.

One day, her Fa said, there would be a Ray who would lead the giraffes out of hiding, tame the tigers, protect the great hives, and lead others out of fear. Then the land would again flow with milk and honey.

>>>

The little train stopped just outside the giraffe's enclosure, and Mum and I got off. Often we sat together on a grassy hill just between the giraffes' and the rhinoceroses' enclosures. It was a great little spot where we could watch the giraffe and all the visitors, most of whom would stand there for a few moments or just keep walking past with only a sideways glance. Fa would say that many people lived their lives like a stroll through the zoo, whatever that meant. On the hill, Mum often went to sleep or was lost somewhere in her thoughts. The giraffe seemed to know when Mum was especially sad and would come over and just look at us. There is something that makes you so peaceful when a giraffe looks at you. Maybe it's the size of its big, watery eyes; or the fact that a giraffe's heart is the biggest of all hearts. A full-grown giraffe's heart weighs twenty-five pounds, as it's required to pump blood all the way up the neck to the giraffe's head. I, on the other hand, was never sad in the zoo. The moment I walked though that gate at the entrance, I was happy. It was like magic.

Giraffe Has Some Fun with the Visitors

That day while I was watching from the little hill and my mother was sleeping, a little boy snuck over the small fence that kept the visitors away from the giraffe's enclosure. He had a large cotton candy in one hand and a water pistol in the other. He started squirting the giraffe with his water pistol. I'd have like to have seen him try that with the elephant. All of a sudden, the giraffe's head shot over the enclosure and scooped the candy floss. It looked like the giraffe had a pink beard.

I was always looking forward to seeing what would happen when people climbed over the low visitors' fence. Later that afternoon, an older man climbed over the fence to get a close-up of the giraffe. Maybe he wasn't that clever, because you can't get a close-up shot of a giraffe. Anyway, over the fence the man went and as he was looking at the LCD screen, the giraffe shot its head over the large fence, opened its mouth amazingly wide, and swallowed both the little man's head and his camera. The man must have wondered why it went dark all of a sudden, or maybe he smelled what the giraffe had for lunch. Anyway, after a few moments, you could see the man panicking and trying to pull himself free. I felt genuinely sorry for the man, but I couldn't help but also be a little bit amused. When the man finally pulled himself free, all his hair was gone. I woke my mum up, and we were soon both beside ourselves laughing on the grass as the little man was shaking his fist at the giraffe while it was leisurely munching on his hairpiece, which Mum called a toupée (which sounds to me like an exotic bird). The giraffe obviously didn't think much of the little brown, dried-up piece of grass and dropped the toupée back over the fence, where the little man snatched it up and no doubt made a beeline for the zoo's exit.

Other visitors could see that the man in his haste had left his camera but nobody after witnessing that incident was willing to go over the fence and retrieve it. I was just about to go and get one of the zookeepers when the giraffe's head came back over, reached down, and picked the camera up in its mouth. I wasn't sure that the giraffe had any right to keep it, but it wouldn't have been easy to catch up to the little man and return it.

Now it's the Chimps' Turn to Have Some Fun

Next time my mum and I came to visit, we watched the chimpanzees in the compound behind the giraffe. They were playing with what looked to be the little man's camera. How they got it, I don't know; perhaps the long-necked giraffe had tired of it and dropped it into the chimps' enclosure to see what they could make of it. Now, chimps are pretty well our closest relatives and are amazing mimics; so in no time at all, they got the hang of the camera. But some people, as they prepare to take a picture of a chimp picking fleas off himself, are just not ready to see a chimp pick up its own camera and take a picture of them, flash and all. Next thing I see is the chimp pointing at the little screen and starting to jump up and down, grinning and laughing hysterically, and what's more, he shows the other chimps the image on the screen and they start to do the very same thing until every chimp is jumping up and down and laughing hysterically. Another man heading for the gate in a hurry.

I don't know how long they'll be able to stay in business if the animals keep this up. It's too human for some people and not the right kind of wild for others. So next time I visited the zoo, the chimp with the camera was nowhere to be seen, and rest were back to arguing and throwing coconuts. Don't tell me this isn't a silly world.

Ray and the Giraffe Become Friends

Mum and I made a routine of visiting the zoo at least twice a week. Mum would rest on that hill as if it were the only place that she could fall asleep and dream. Meanwhile, I would tell Giraffe the stories that Fa and I told to each other. Giraffe would come over and listen, more, it seemed, to the sound of my voice; but whenever a giraffe showed up in the story, Giraffe clearly paid more attention. I even made up some new stories where the giraffe was kinder to young boys and men without hair, although secretly I was drawn to mischief. When Giraffe especially liked the story, he would reach over the fence and put his head beside mine and he'd let me rub his nose lightly; but most of all, Giraffe liked it when I rubbed the back of his neck good and hard.

Then one day when I was reaching behind Giraffe and rubbing its neck, Giraffe reached behind my neck and with its big lips began to gently rub my neck at the same time! It was a little scary at first, but I trusted the gentleness of Giraffe and so eventually relaxed and enjoyed the massage. Todd the zookeeper saw this happening and came over to us. I thought, *Oh, Oh, we're perhaps not supposed to be here on the hill between the compounds*, but he told me that he had for some time been concerned that the zoo was not able to locate another young orphan giraffe to keep this orphan company. Giraffes need the company of their own kind. He went on to say that what the giraffe and I had been doing was called necking. I giggled and went red, but the zookeeper assured me that many animals with longer necks and manes, like giraffes and horses, seal friendships that way. Todd said that he had seen us coming regularly and that we were welcome to sit between the enclosures on the hill whenever we liked.

Tum's Story

All through the summer, Mum and I came to the zoo at least twice a week--mostly to visit Giraffe. Then on the last day the zoo was open for the season, we went to say goodbye to him. Mum and I sat on the hill in the rain all day. Todd the zookeeper came over and told us the story of how they had rescued the young giraffe when the King of Zaire had sent his army to kill the animals and collect the skins so he could sell them to earn money to buy weapons to keep the people in fear. The king was always dressed in tiger skins and called himself Mobutu: the Tiger King. His troops were not allowed to hunt tigers, but as there were fewer and fewer animals for the tigers to eat, they began to turn on people.

Todd went on to say that before the Tiger King there was a man called Patrice Lumumba, who was the leader of the Giraffe Party. Lumumba was a man of great wisdom and foresight, but he did not survive. When all was lost to the Tiger Party, a team from IAFA (International Fund for Animal Welfare) managed a daring rescue of a young giraffe, which was the symbol for this peaceful political party. When asked why they had risked their lives to rescue the giraffe, one of them said, "We must keep hope alive."

The young giraffe's name is Tumaini, which means "hope" in Swahili. "We just call him Tum, though," Todd concluded. "So you can see Tum is a very special giraffe and has a very special purpose."

Todd's story was not exactly the same as my favourite story, but they were similar in some important ways. If it was possible I loved the giraffe Tum even more, knowing his story. I always believed Fa's stories, even though Mum would sometimes roll her eyes. Of course, I would not believe all of what Fa said.

Once I questioned Fa, asking him if that really happened? He said, "Of course it did, but exaggeration is the very heart and soul of story. Stories exaggerate what's most important in life, so it stands out against what is meaningless."

This is not what Mrs. MacFiercesome believed. She felt that exaggeration was the enemy of good writing and was determined to stamp it out. Many of the kids in my class laughed when I told them Fa's stories.

"That's only a story and it's not true," they would say.

On the other hand, I felt that it was *only stories that really were true*, and of course whatever happened at Wednesday's show and tell. Mostly I felt sad for my classmates because stories meant so much to me, and I couldn't imagine my life without them.

Last Day at the Zoo

Todd and Mum went off, and I was left on the little hill with Tum. In the past few months, as I told stories to Tum and we rubbed each other's necks, I began to hear Tum's thoughts in my own head. In those moments, we seemed to be able to communicate without words.

Today was going to be our last day together for a long time. The zoo was closing for the winter. Mum and I had knitted a very long scarf for Tum. Todd let us into Tum's enclosure, and we wrapped it round and round Tum's neck. I was crying and laughing at the same time. In my mind, I could hear Tum say that he had given a gift as well but that I would not know what is was for a while. I wrapped my arms around Tum's beautiful neck and we said goodbye to each other. It seemed like it would be forever until the first day of spring when the zoo opened again. Both Mum and Todd held my hand as we walked together toward the Big Gate. At the Big Gate, Todd reached into his pack and gave me a camera. I was quite surprised to see that camera again.

"Isn't that the camera the chimps were using for a while?" I asked.

"Yes, one of the chimps handed it back to me after he'd grown tired of it, and I found a few pictures of some very surprised zoo visitors; but most of the pictures were of you and Tum. So that's how I knew the camera was meant for you."

I remembered what Fa had said about how life was always an exchange, even if the exchange was a prayer, a whispered blessing, or a small offering. Fa said, "You must try never to take anything without giving something back."

So I reached into my bag and brought out a dried bumblebee. This was my and Fa's other favourite animal. "Don't forget the small things," Fa would say.

The bee was precious to me, and I handed it gently to Todd.

"*Bee* gentle," I reminded him, emphasizing the bee.

"*Bee* good," Todd said back.

We laughed and hugged. "See you in the spring!" Todd called out as Mum and I walked through the Big Gate.

CHAPTER TWO
THE QUEST BECOMES CLEAR

Golden Grove Aviaries

We were both quiet as we climbed into the old blue Volvo. Bees were still on my mind, so I suggested that Mum and I visit Golden Grove Aviary, since it was on our way home. Aviary is a fancy name for a bee farm, and Golden Grove Aviary is where Fa and I would pick up our honey after visiting the zoo. Mum agreed, and so off we went to Golden Grove.

We were driving up and down hills when I spotted some comfrey plants along the side of the road. Mum stopped, and I dug one of them up and put it in a small cloth bag. We then drove on until I saw the small golden arch at the entrance of Golden Grove Aviaries. The owners were also the beekeepers and they greeted us like old friends. They took us down to the storeroom, where Mum and I got to sample the many varieties of honey: clover, alfalfa, buckwheat, wildflower, and orange blossom honey; and many other strange ones, such as basswood honey. Some as golden as sunlight; others dark like moonbeams, all rich and sweet, full of subtle tastes of the earth, the fields, and the flowers.

I thought back to the time when the beekeepers had left Fa and me alone in this storeroom. We were filling up a large jar of wildflower honey from the big vat. I got to pull the lever that opened the honey gate. But because the honey flowed in slow motion, you had to close the gate just before the jar was full. I was mesmerized by the golden flowing honey and I closed the gate a bit too late. The jar filled to the brim and a single drop fell from the lip. Fa caught the drop in his hand and he licked it off as though it were priceless.

But because the jar was filled to the brim, we could not put the lid on. I could always tell when Fa got an idea that was a little mischievous--a certain look would pass across his face, as it did just then. Fa looked over one shoulder and then the other, winked at me, then put the jar up to his lips and took a great big gulp, sucking the honey down. He stood there for a moment, eyes rolled skyward, then handed me the jar. I did the same--looked over my shoulders and then raised the jar to my lips and drank the heavy golden sunshine. I saw a burst of white light and my knees almost gave way. I handed Fa back the jar, and we silently nodded to each other. Fa always paid more for the honey than the beekeepers asked. He said that honey was worth so much more. Fa also knew that at Golden Grove the beekeepers made sure they left plenty of honey behind for the bees to survive the winter.

The First Hive is in Peril

As Mum was having tea with the beekeepers, I went out toward the hives and planted the comfrey plant, which I know bees like. I felt the energy of the hum as I got close to the hives. I was not afraid of the bees, as most of them were from the European variety and were not at all aggressive. There was a single bee that was buzzing near my ear as I replanted the comfrey. At first I gently waved it away, next I told it to buzz off, but the bee was persistent. After a little while, I began to notice a pattern to the buzzes. I knew the pattern meant something; the bee was trying to communicate with me. At first it was slow, but I found I could decode the buzzing sounds. The buzzing has distinct tones or notes, and the gift from Tum was that I was given the ability to understand what these notes meant to bees.

While still surprised that I could understand what the bee was saying, the bee began telling me its story.

"I am one of the few African bees and I have come from a mighty hive that we bees call "The First Hive." It is the hive of the Queen of Queens. All the queen bees in Africa come from this First Hive, and all bees can be traced back to this one hive. Given that bees pollinate more than 60 percent of the world's plants, its very existence and location must be kept secret. If this hive ever fell into hostile hands, then all life would be in jeopardy."

"And," I replied, "If anyone was able to control this hive, they could control the destiny of life on this planet."

"That's it exactly," said the bee. "The Tiger King has been determined to find the First Hive. If he succeeds, he will enslave the Queen of Queens and would seek to control all life on this planet. Someone must let the Queen of Queens know and prevent the Tiger King from discovering the location of the First Hive."

Ray sat there, stunned; she knew the planet was in trouble with global warming, with pollution, with factory farming, with over-consumption. She was trying to do all the small things she could to help; she even knew there had been a sharp decline in honeybees, and she knew this was the greatest peril yet but she did not know why and how. Now she did, but how could she tell anybody?

"Oh, this is what the bees told me," she'd say, and it would this give the girls at school another reason to laugh . . . who wouldn't laugh?

Ray Deceives Her Mum for the Greater Good

Ray knew that Tum wouldn't laugh at this story, but how to visit the zoo when it was closed? Her mother would not let her, but she envisioned that mischievous glint in her father's eye and knew that Fa would have been in favour of trying.

Ray found out that in summer, there's a bus that goes right to the zoo, but in winter, that bus dead-ends at Sheppard Ave. But from the turnaround on Meadowvale, she could hike along the Rouge River and into the back of the zoo. Google Earth was a good deal of help here, and she and Fa had often hiked in the Rouge before or after their visits to the zoo. They had names for many places; such as the place where the birds eat from your hands, or the place of the flat rocks, or deer dens, or the place of five sunsets--which was a ridge with five ledges so you could run up to one ledge and see the sunset and then run up to the next and see the sun set again and get five sunsets in one evening. Fa said that he felt diminished by every sunset he missed. This is a way we can make up for them, I said, and so we did.

>>>

On a really hot day, Fa and I would put on our oldest running shoes and do a river hike up the Rouge. Do you know what we found over and over again, along the banks of the river, bobbing along? Golf balls, yes, but would you believe . . . hundreds of coconuts? Those Chimps!

So I typed up a form that said I was going on a winter excursion to the zoo on a school day and I asked my mum to sign it. She took a glance at it and saw "zoo" and "field trip."

"Do they want me to come along dear?" she asked.

"Not this time, Mum."

And so Mum just signed it. Then I took the form to school but I knew my teacher would read it more carefully, so I had put in smaller lettering that it was an Independent Study Program with the Ancillary Department of the Zoo (I'd heard the word "ancillary," and it means just about anything, so I thought it'd be a good word to use). I had done a summer program with the zoo, so it was not too much of a stretch.

I was sweating as my teacher was reading it. I was pretty sure it had no spelling mistakes, but would it pass her eagle eye?

"That sounds interesting," she finally said. "Would you do an oral report to the class on your winter visit to the zoo?"

Well, I hadn't expected that but I said, "Of course, Mrs. MacFiercesome."

She was nicer than her name suggests.

Now you might be wondering how I could do such a mischievous thing. Mind you, I wasn't lying, but there was some deception involved, which my mum would say amounted to the same thing as lying. It was one of the very few things I secretly didn't agree with Mum about. But I believe that with any deception there must be a really good cause; it can't be just to get something you want--like a new iPod. It must be what Fa said was for the Greater Good. If it's for self-interest then it's the same as lying, and mum's right. But this was to save the bees and the first hive and all living things, and so I decided to do what must be done--as long as it didn't hurt anyone else, and it was for the Greater Good.

The Unauthorized Field Trip to the Zoo

So when the day of my "field trip" finally came, I was as prepared as I could be. Just outside the house, I sat down on the steps. Fa always did this before heading off on trips. This was a cultural practice that he'd picked up on an extended trip to Siberia. While I sat there, I realized I had forgotten one or two things, one being an offering for the spirits of the forest, so I ran back inside. When Mum, Fa, and I went out for our little adventures together, Fa would often say, "Every time we step out of the house there's a chance that we won't return, even if we're just going for milk."

"Really!" Mum would say. "Is that appropriate for an eleven-year-old to know?"

Well, I suppose it was true, but I hoped in this case it was not.

I took the bus to Meadowvale and was the only person left on the bus as it stopped at the end of the line. The bus driver looked at me strangely as I got off, so I said, "I'm studying the Wintering Habits of Owls in the

Rouge Valley."

It was true sort of true, as I was going to visit a spot that Fa and I called The Hoot. But I discovered if you put what you were doing in a kind of official language, the way educated people do, then everything becomes somehow all right. Well, it seemed to work on the bus driver, as he just nodded his head and wished me luck.

I walked along the Rouge River on the ice. I was careful to carry a thick, long stick, as I'd been taught. If I did fall through, even though I knew it was a shallow river, I could use the stick as a lever to pull myself up with. Fa taught me never to go onto the ice without a big strong stick and hold it like a tightrope walker. Fa had about as many stories of going through the ice as you could shake a stick at (that was another of his expressions). Like the time he was unhappy as a teenager because there was a girl he liked who didn't seem to like him. I can't imagine anyone not liking Fa, but it's his story.

Fa Goes Through the Ice

Fa was on a school trip to the Rocky Mountains just outside of somewhere called Jasper. It was wintertime, and everyone set out from the camp on an organized hike into the woods. There were some pretty strict rules about staying with the group; however, Fa dragged behind and then snuck off into the woods. He bushwhacked, which means not sticking to a trail, until he came to a big river. It was covered with ice, and so he started to walk out on it. He knew he shouldn't, as it was sure to be running fast and deep underneath him. But boys do some pretty nutty things when they're not able to express their feelings. So he walked out onto the unsafe ice. Somewhere near the middle it gave way. Fa said, "It's not a slow cracking and then a leisurely descent into the water. It happens in an instant; you don't even have a chance to put your arms out--even if that would help."

Then like his other ice stories, he said, "There's no way to pull yourself up onto the ice, as it just keeps breaking around you. That's where the stick comes in handy. It gives you something to pull yourself up with and it extends out onto stronger ice."

Fa sees this as the lesson in his stories. I think there are others, but anyway, Fa shot through the ice and was instantly under the water . . . freezing-cold mountain water, silent and swift. He looked up and the little circle of light that he fell though was by the second disappearing as he was being swept away under the ice. There was no possibility of swimming back to the opening. *This was it*, Fa thought. Absolutely nothing could be done. He calls this "being in between adventures." One adventure's over and the other one hasn't quite begun yet. Then all of a sudden he was in the open river, out from under the ice, in huge rapids that had standing waves of nearly two storeys high, or so Fa said. Even if you account for exaggeration, that would mean a standing wave of one storey high, which is twelve feet, and that's still a mighty big rapid.

Anyway, now Fa's being swept along in the rapids and he sees that below the rapids, the river disappears under the ice again. He only has a brief moment of time before he's lost again. This is his big chance, so he said that he became the mighty salmon that takes on this river each spring.

With salmon-like strength he swims across the current and makes it to shore just before the river would have taken him under the ice again. He lies gasping on shore, unable to move, every muscle completely exhausted. His heavy winter clothing begins to freeze to the ground and lock him into an icy coffin. Fa just manages to move a little bit at a time, crawling the couple of miles back to the empty camp. He puts some logs on the coals in the fireplace and feels lucky to be alive.

The lesson of the story, Fa says, is to carry a big, strong stick--and on an adventure, it is often the most unlikely things that come to your aid-- like the rapids. That's not all of what I take from the story, but I still carry a big, strong stick when I walk on ice.

The Hoot

I soon arrived at a bend in the river where a path led to a clearing in the middle of the woods. In the centre of the clearing stood a huge, mostly dead sycamore tree. It was a favourite meeting spot for owls, which are usually solitary. It's the place Fa and I called *The Hoot.*

Fa said, "People are one of three things: *Guardians, Sleepers,* or *Takers.* Guardians take on the responsibility to protect something they love or care about. Takers look out for themselves--always grabbing and never being able to get enough. Sleepers don't know who they are yet--they could wake to their Guardianship or they could fall and become Takers. There are animal species which are also either Guardians, Sleepers, or Takers. Giraffes, for instance, are Guardians as a species, and tigers are Takers as a species. But it also varies within a species: you might get a Tiger who behaves like a Guardian and a Giraffe that behaves like a Taker.

"Humans began," Fa said, "as Takers. We stole life from every other living thing to maintain our own lives. Our species flourished, but often at the expense of other species. Even though our species were Takers, there have always been some of us who were Guardians. *Now, because of our increasing numbers, we need to evolve into a Guardian species.*"

Owls are both Takers and Guardians. I walked into the clearing and sat down under the old sycamore, a distant cousin of the cypress tree, which is the name everyone other than Fa calls me. Names are powerful things, and so I spoke to the tree and told it my given name.

"I am Cypress; my true name is Ray. I know you as Sycamore. You are the old one who has seen back to a time before even my great-grandmother; you have seen the river change its course many times; you have known children playing in your branches."

I saw bits of old rope and a rotted plank high up in its branches. I hoped it was official enough sounding for an old one like the Sycamore and also said with enough feeling to have a good result. I took out a little pouch from my backpack, dug a small hole in the ground at the foot of the great tree, and put some coffee beans in the hole as an offering to the Sycamore as the elder of the forest. I read that Native people use tobacco as an offering, but Mum and Fa love their coffee, so I figure coffee beans would work, too. That way, I won't get caught with tobacco and get into even more trouble than I am already in.

As I was burying the beans, I felt something very large right behind me. I saw a shadow move across the snow in front of me and felt a breeze that made all the hairs on my body stand at attention, but there was no sound. Whatever it was, it was silent. Then, a moment later, a large snowy owl flew in a circle around me and the tree, once and then again, obviously observing me, observing my every move, and perhaps even my thoughts.

Owls' feathers happen to be shaped in such a way that they create very little turbulence in the air as they fly. It is the turbulence that creates the whooshing sound that can alert prey and humans to their presence. To reduce the turbulence, an owl's feathers are grouped together into comb-like flutings. These flutings create micro-turbulences that effectively muffle the sound of the air rushing over the wing surface, allowing the owl to fly silently. It may well be that owls are not silent, but rather the flutings actually shift the sound energy created by the wingbeats to a higher-frequency spectrum that most creatures (including prey and humans) cannot hear.

The snowy owl landed in the tree just above me. Soon after that, I heard the words, "You may pass." The words were so distinct and the voice was so clear that I looked around to see where it came from, but no one was there--just me, the owl, and the tree. The voice was spoken into my mind; or maybe it was at another frequency, I don't know, but I did know that I had permission to pass from the *Guardian of the Woods.*

I walked back to the river, picked up my stick, and continued on toward the zoo. I didn't know how I would get through the dense, tangled forest that lay on the other side of the river. And I was even less sure how I would travel through all the other animal enclosures to the giraffe's indoor barn or how I would get into the barn to talk with Tum. I had decided to tell one friend about my "field trip" so someone would know where to look for me if I didn't return home that night. But the minute I told my friend Zoë, I regretted it. Her first response was something that I hadn't thought of, probably because I had always seen the woods and its inhabitants as my other home; a home that if treated with care and respect would embrace me. But I found to my shock that others had very different feelings toward nature and the forest; for them it was a place of fear and danger . . . a place where the twisted outcasts of society were exiled along with all the other beasts waiting to rip you to shreds after terrorizing you. Their relationships with the woods were through horror films.

Zoë's immediate reaction was, "Climbing fences in the zoo, that sounds like a bad idea--what if you climb into the tigers' enclosure? From the back of the zoo, how would you know what you're climbing into?"

I had to admit, this wasn't simply a knee-jerk horror film reaction, but a reasonable concern. Finally, I decided that the stakes were high enough and that I had to speak with Tum, but that I would somehow do it without climbing fences. But how was I going to get into the zoo during the winter, when it was closed, without climbing fences?

I admit I didn't know as I set out, but on any adventure, Fa would say, "The way is never clear from the start it only makes sense when you look back on it. You just have to make the path by walking it. If it's a sure thing, then there's no adventure."

If there was one thing that Fa knew above all else, it was how to free himself from the bonds of everyday life and set off on an adventure. Well, I had permission to pass from the *Guardian of the Forest*, and that had to count for something.

The Abandoned Monorail

I kept looking in the direction of the zoo for anything unusual or any kind of assistance. I had thought of the small train and the tracks but it only ran inside the zoo proper--not in the wilderness surrounding the zoo, and certainly not from the back. Yet there was something that seemed to weave like a snake through the dense woods. I climbed an old white pine with a forked branch nearly to the top where I could get a good look at the other side of the river and into the zoo. Sure enough, it was just like a giant snake that went up and down and curved this way and that through the tangled woods and wild part of the zoo, and the tail of the snake looked like it was just around the next bend in the river. Fa had told me about the monorail, but I didn't know that once it was abandoned they would just leave the cement causeway in the woods. Fa said that a fatal accident in the first week of operation doomed the new monorail. This happened before I was born.

I could walk right into what was once a monorail station. Tangled vines covered the walls so I could hardly make out the station's name. I cleared some vines and rubbed the dust off the wall. Underneath it were shiny tiles that had "River Station" printed on them. It was like being in some futuristic movie where there are no people left on earth, and nature is once again taking its course and reclaiming all our concrete and steel. It was like a vision of the future if I did not succeed on my quest!

I began walking along the monorail path. They had a long time ago removed the steel rail but the cement causeway still snaked through the forest, sometimes rising up above the trees and giving me an excellent vantage point. Soil had built up on the cement, and plants had taken root. It was an amazing path, a green-carpeted walkway into the sky--worth the trip in itself.

"Trust in your own Destiny," Fa would say; "that's the most important kind of trust."

Well, so far I hadn't had to climb any fences--the monorail created a path through the dense forest and lifted me over the fences and across the enclosures, out of reach of even the tigers. After a good hour of hiking, I saw my familiar little hill, and behind it was Tum's wintering place (or as Todd called it, the Large Ungulates Barn). I climbed off the monorail track and onto a small path to the back of the animal barn. I saw a shadow cross my path and I looked up. The Snowy Owl swooped and dipped low and then flapped hard and climbed back into the blue sky.

Arrival at the Large Ungulates Barn

I could feel my heart grow as I got close to the barn. My heart felt as big as a giraffe's heart. Would the barn be locked? It was. I raced around it, checking for other entrances. There was a large hanger door for the ungulates like Tum to come in and out of, but it was opened with a large winch that I could not even turn. However, I had not come this far to be denied. I peered through one of the small windows, and saw someone moving inside. I banged as loud as I could on the window, the figure started toward the door. It was Todd! He looked pretty surprised to see me. He paused for a second and then pointed around toward the side door.

It was pretty confusing as Todd opened the door. Somehow, from across the large barn, Tum knew that it was me. I could feel pressure waves against my skin, even though there was no sound. These waves created an intense feeling all over my skin and inside me. At the same time, Todd had lots of questions for me, which I could not hear very well because I was overwhelmed with feelings. Bless his heart, Todd noticed my emotions and said, "Go and see Tum, we can talk afterwards."

What a reunion it was. I just wrapped my arms around Tum's neck and wept. Tum flapped his ears this way and that, which is how giraffes and elephants show emotions. I told Tum the whole story of the Bees and how the Dark King Mobutu was using the Tigers to find the First Hive and if he did, he would control the propagation of sixty percent of all living things. Tum understood the seriousness of this. But giraffes are not prone to rash decisions, so Tum just stood there with his legs slightly splayed out and the hump at the bottom of its neck pushed upwards, swaying back and forth.

Giraffes are usually gentle, as they are one of the Guardian Species, but it is a myth that they are always so. If their family or one of the herd is threatened, they will come to each other's assistance and swing their muscled necks against their adversaries, knocking them like golf balls thirty or forty feet in the air. This does not kill them, but it does make any predator think twice about attacking. I felt very safe as Tum was now in a protective stance while we both were thinking of what should be done next.

The Way Forward

Finally, Tum said, "You must let the Queen of Queens know of the peril she and the other Queens are in."

"How am I going to get to Africa? And even if I did, Africa's a very big place, and no one knows the location of the First Hive."

"That is true," said Tum, "but as Guardians to the True King and as his Listeners, we know many things; not the exact location of the hive, but we do know it's in the Kalahari."

"That's where the Bushmen live," I jumped in. "Fa told me a story about a Bushman named Xhabbo who was one of his closest friends and how they had journeyed from New York City to the Heart of Africa to visit one of the world greatest witch doctors."

"Well that narrows it down quite a bit," said Tum.

"But getting into the zoo in winter is quite different than finding a truly secret place in the heart of Africa," I replied. "And finding one of

Dad's friends is like trying to catch the wind."

"Don't forget your gift," said Tum; "you are a Listener now, you can hear thoughts and talk with nature in a language that has been forgotten by most humans. This will give you much assistance along the way and help you find what others can't. Ray, you will also discover another gift that will help you on your next quest."

"Another gift that people will no doubt laugh at," I said, and then immediately regretted it. "I do appreciate the gifts, Tum, I really do--but why do they have to be hidden ones? Why not something like an iron body, or incredible strength, or the ability to fly, or even spin webs. Boys seem to get these great gifts, while girls get hidden gifts that you can't show off, and if you speak of them to others, you get laughed at. I'd rather be a boy hero."

"Someone who needs to be seen as a hero is not a true hero," Tum replied.

"I guess I knew that but sometimes I wish it were different, that's all."

Tum reached down with his head and gently knocked me over into the hay. "We all do from time to time."

I grabbed onto the ossicones on top of Tum's head, which are bony protuberances to protect the head. Tum lifted me off the ground as I hung on.

When Tum let me down I asked if he thought Xhabbo was important. "Very," was Tum's reply.

Now it was time to say goodbye to Tum, but this time it was with joy. Our friendship was sealed, my quest was clear, and we'd "stolen" a visit, so I knew that we never needed to be too long apart.

CHAPTER THREE
THE DECEPTION GROWS

A Few Drops of Deception

Occasionally, Fa would drop by the school and take me out on an adventure. I'd say, "Shouldn't we tell Mum or let Mrs. MacFiercesome know what we're doing?"

He'd say, "Keep some of your plans secret. You spread them too thin, and they lose power before you're even out the door. So let others know only on a need-to-know basis. Then, if you need to alter your plans, you can--without confusing others who think in a more linear fashion."

Well, it was time to speak to Todd, and I guess this advice applied now. I told Todd that I missed my Fa (which was certainly true) and needed to see Tum. He seemed to understand.

"How did you get in here?" he asked. "The big fences are impossible to scale, the main gate is well guarded, and passkeys are required to go anywhere. In winter, it's a Fort Knox for animals."

I told him about the Snowy Owl and the abandoned monorail.

"That's brilliant," he said. "I can't give you a pass for the main gate, but I suppose it's all right to give you a passkey for the Large Ungulates Barn. I could still get into trouble for this, but these keys are less restricted."

I thanked Todd very much and reached up to give him a hug. I offered him the rest of the coffee beans as I left, which he genuinely appreciated.

I returned to the monorail track, followed that until I was off zoo property, and then back along the river. Even though I was on a tight schedule to get home on time, I still stopped at *The Hoot* to say goodbye to the Sycamore and thank the Guardian Owl for safe passage.

Fa told me that Henry David Thoreau, one of his favourite authors, had hiked for over an hour during the winter to a clearing in the woods just to keep a meeting he had with an elder beech tree. So there was nothing crazy about thanking a sycamore, or even a cypress, from time to time.

I walked back in the door at home just in time not to arouse any suspicion. Mum was there to greet me. "How was your winter field trip to the zoo?" she asked.

Convincing Mum

Now, I love my mum more than anyone else, and she is my Guardian; there's nothing she wouldn't do to protect me. If I were stuck under a car, I have no doubt that my mum would take on superpowers and lift that car. But if my mum senses danger, then she puts a halt to things. Even if I would have been able to convince her of how important this quest was, she would sense danger and jam on the emergency brakes. It's hard for mums to think of the *Greater Good* when it conflicts with the safety of their daughters. This is where Fas come in; as far as they are concerned, we girls can more often than not do a thing, as long as it doesn't have anything to do with boys. That's one thing they don't trust. I wonder why that is?

So the hardest thing to do was not to spill the beans and just tell Mum everything. Instead I told a *White Lie*: that's the kind that serves the *Greater Good*.

"Mum, hasn't it been good going to the Zoo over the summer?"

"Yes, darling; why are you asking?"

"Even the trip to the aviary was fun, wasn't it?"

"Yes of course," she said with a growing suspicion.

"What-about-a-trip-to-Africa-to-see-the-Bushmen," I blurted out.

Oh no, I thought, *that sounded insane--I might as well have said, "Let's go to Saturn and visit the rings."* But Mother is very clever; she was more interested in why all of a sudden I wanted to go to Africa to visit the Bushmen. Warning, warning . . . Mum's on to something.

What would Fa have done? He had been in this situation many times. Fa would say, "When you lose a person's trust, it takes a long time to get it back--so never allow yourself to get caught in a lie. This is where the art of misdirection comes in, and misdirection is not a lie."

I could sense the thin ice here but decided to go ahead anyway.

"Do you miss Fa?" I asked.

"Of course I do, darling, and I know you do as well. I'm so proud of you and how you are going through this."

My knees were a bit weak, but this was no time to turn back. I pressed on.

"Well, I know someone who knows where Fa might be," I announced.

It had the anticipated effect on Mum. Her face clearly registered surprise, and for a moment, she was lost for words.

Finally she said, "Who? Who?"

"Mum, you sound like an owl."

"This is no time for joking."

Which really meant that I'd caught her attention.

"Xhabbo," I said.

"Xhabbo," Mum said out loud, clearly pondering the thought.

"Xhabbo could lead us to the Witch Doctor and the Witch Doctor might be able to tell us where Fa is. "

In the past I'd ask Fa for the story of Xhabbo and the Witch Doctor over and over again. But I knew it was not one of Mum's favourites. I think she suspected he'd made it up. So I knew that I had to deal with this.

"Mum, if Xhabbo exists, then it's likely the Witch Doctor exists, right? And if Xhabbo and the Witch Doctor exist, then it's also possible that the Witch Doctor is as powerful as Fa said, right? And if the Witch Doctor is as powerful as that, then there's a chance he'll know where Fa is."

"That's a lot of ifs and maybes," Mum noted.

But I could see that the logic was appealing to her.

"Yes, there are a lot of ifs, but we have to at least try to find Fa, right? And wouldn't it be incredible to go to Africa over Christmas! And it won't be expensive, because no one thinks of going to Africa at Christmas."

There was a long pause. I held my breath.

"Okay," she finally said, "on one condition."

Here comes the proviso, I thought. *It'll be something like: "Don't get into trouble," or "You have to keep up with your homework."*

"On one condition," she repeated: "that you track down Xhabbo in New York, or wherever, and he agrees to take us."

This was a pretty big condition, but one step at a time, and maybe it would give me the chance to discover what that other gift was.

CHAPTER FOUR
THE BUSHMAN: MASTER COMMUNICATORS

Searching For Xhabbo

I searched for Xhabbo using all the search engines and all the social networking sites, but somehow I couldn't see Xhabbo on Facebook. I got the NYC phonebook online, and as a first or last name, there was no Xhabbo (thank goodness it wasn't Jones or Wong). I didn't leave a stone unturned. I searched everywhere. I posted on blogs, I talked to the Webmasters at Kalahari.com, dot org, and dot net. Bushmen.com, dot org, and dot net. Fa sometimes used the name "!Kung San peoples," so I tried this and found very little information online. All to no avail. Christmas was fast approaching, and so was the two-week window in which to book our tickets. I needed another strategy.

"When the bone does not seem to be buried where you're digging, then don't just keep on digging; start digging another hole," Fa would say.

This is not as easy as it sounds, especially when you're not sure where to start the next hole. In school they called it lateral thinking. I was a master at this; it was straight line thinking that sometimes got the better of me.

I wanted to communicate with Xhabbo.

"We nearly always see communication as language," Fa would say. "Yet, verbal communication is just a fraction of what we communicate, the tip of the iceberg." I remember Fa quoting Sigmund Freud, "Even though the lips are silent the body oozes betrayal from every pore."

This, I think, is a must-know if you are going to be successful on your adventures. I am practising to make my body ooze a little less betrayal.

Hidden Languages of the Forest

Once in the woods while I was standing in a circle that I'd drawn observing everything on that small scale, I noticed thirteen slugs in the grass, separated by a few feet, which would have been like miles for them; I saw them converge together to cross over a very dry spot of earth. Obviously they were maintaining moisture by becoming one big, wet slug. Then on the other side, they separated and headed out independently. How did they let each other know where they were going to meet? I went online and found that there's no scientific explanation for how many animals communicate, and that similar slugs to the ones I witnessed are a special problem. How do starlings all change directions instantaneously, without causing mid-air, multi-bird collisions?

A term biologists use for communication that they don't understand is *morphic resonance*. It was fascinating to read about how many mysteries there are in animal-to-animal or insect-to-insect communication. When the big tsunami hit Southeast Asia, it's now clear that days before, before all our forecasts told us of the tsunami, there were mass migrations of animals from the coast to farther inland. There is this immense web of communications of which humans see only this little part of the web they inhabit.

"Has it always been this way?" I asked Fa.

Fa looked at me more than a little bit surprised that I'd investigated this. He paused as though weighing whether he should tell me something; which he rarely did, much to Mum's chagrin.

The Bushmen: First of the First Peoples

"The Bushmen," Fa began, "were likely the First of the First Peoples. The original *Homo sapiens*. They are special in a secret way. They still know the language of most of the animals of the deserts and forests of the Kalahari. All their senses speak to them. This was how the Bushmen used their brains over the millennia: they used them to understand all the living things around them, rather than create technology. So the Bushmen use very few tools and own only what they can carry. They had no Iron Age or Computer Age or Information Age, but they can speak to ants as well as antelopes, to the honey badger and the honeybee. They speak through song, through dance, through story, and even in silence. The drum, the djembe, occupies a special place for the Bushmen; it is a being in itself that they communicate with. They appear simple and innocent but they are master communicators, beyond all other humans on the earth. They call their Kalahari 'The Speaking Land.'

"When the first humans migrated north from the heart of Africa, they began to fashion tools. This was the branch of humans that followed the path of technology rather than communication. Now we humans with tools are finally entering the Communications Age. But the Bushmen, the !Kung San people, have never left this age. I thought that perhaps it might be possible to combine our technology with their ability to communicate with all forms of life. It would give me a chance to correct some of the flaws of the Internet by creating a larger EcoNet, which would be an Internet for all living beings [Fa had been on the team at ARPAnet in the early days of the Internet, but he had left it as it evolved into a military technology]. This would make it much harder for us as a species to exploit the natural world and its inhabitants, as we would be confronted with the stories of their suffering and would be compelled to change our behaviour."

Fa concluded, "This is really why I went to Africa to see the Great Witch Doctor--to ask for his help in this."

Remembering this conversation with Fa helped in that there might be another way to communicate with Xhabbo. Fa had brought back a small djembe for me from Africa. It was handmade, of course, and Fa had said it was very special in that the drum skin was not goat--as is usually the case--it was made from the skin of a giraffe; in fact, the sides of the drum were covered in golden hair with large, white spots. At first I was horrified, until Fa said the Bushmen would never kill a giraffe--it is the most sacred animal to the !Kung San. But animals of course die naturally, and the !Kung San know when this is happening. They travel great distances to where the giraffe is dying and even offer a medicine to the dying giraffe that makes its passage between worlds easier. Then, with the herd, they share in the grief.

Learning to Drum

So every evening after I'd done my homework, I went out to the fire circle behind the house and would just drum. We're outside the city limits and are allowed open fires. Fa insisted that we live somewhere that allowed open fires. So we have a great stone fire circle, and around it is a straw-bale wall covered in clay slip with all sorts of nooks in it for important objects. We live at the top of Mt. Albert, which is really a big hill, so we look down on the forested valley around us. The big, round log seats are in a circle between the low wall and the fire. The wall protects you from the wind and reflects back the heat of the fire.

Ma and Fa had many drum and story gatherings around this fire, so the neighbours are used to feasts, ceremonies, and impromptu concerts. But it has never been a typical "party" house. There is rarely any alcohol, as First peoples are often present, and out of respect for "the shadow of alcohol in their community," as Fa put it, we rarely have alcohol at our gatherings. Our neighbours at first thought we were weird and flaky (and maybe they still think so), but because of our influence they've become a bit more weird and flaky themselves--so now the difference is a less noticeable.

Mum would tell me that all music arises out of the silence of the heart. So I would start by just sitting around the fire and listening. Listening to the sounds of the fire, the night, and the beat of my own heart, I then let the music flow from my hands into the drum, into the night and back to my heart and to my hands again, in a circle, over and over again. Sometimes a song or prayer would just arise from my heart spontaneously and I would sing to the night and to the wintering birds, and the blanket of stars and the snowy owl in the distance. At no time was my intention of seeing Xhabbo far from my thoughts or my hands or my song. I did this night after night, never wavering in my intention. After four or five nights, I got into the rhythm of it. No longer was it a struggle or an effort; I felt that I could do it forever, every night. But a fire every night was taking its toll on our woodpile, which needed to last till the spring. Mum did not say anything, as she sensed that I was doing something important, in a way that I was not used to doing things.

Xhabbo Hears the Call

It was a computer voice on the phone: "Will you accept a collect call from . . ." there's silence and then more silence. The computer repeated, "Will you accept a collect call from . . ." again more silence. Some of Fa's friends were pretty weird when it came to computers and technology, so on a hunch, I just said, "Yes, I'll accept the charges."

"Hello, hello," I heard the voice say. "You must be Ray."

The voice at the other end knew my secret name.

"Is your mother there?"

"No she's working late tonight," I replied.

"Well, I'm at the airport and I've come into town for a storytelling Festival called 'Listen Up.'"

I knew the festival well; Fa had performed in it many times. It's where Fa and Ma met.

Growing more curious, I asked, "What's your name?"

"Xhabbo," was the reply.

"Xhabbo," I relished the name. "I've been expecting you."

"Do you have a place for me to stay for a few days while I'm in town? Do you need to ask your mother when she returns?"

"No," I quickly replied, "I'm sure it would be okay with Mum."

After a warm exchange, in which Xhabbo said how much he loved Fa and was looking forward to meeting Mum and me, Xhabbo handed the phone back to the taxi driver, and I gave him directions on how to bring Xhabbo to our house from the airport.

"Stop calling it coincidence," Fa would often say. "Never use that word, there's no such thing, never has been, and hopefully never will be. Fate, maybe; destiny, certainly."

An hour later, Xhabbo arrived. It was hard not to tell him everything right away and discover if it was possible for him to accompany us to the Kalahari to find the Witch Doctor to aid in my Quest, and to discover more about Fa. What was vital was to get help in finding the First Hive and to warn the Queen of Queens.

When Mum arrived home from work, she was unaware that Xhabbo was already unpacking in the spare room. It was so great to see the surprise on her face when she came face to face with Xhabbo in the dark upstairs hallway. Face to face is not the right phrase in this case. Xhabbo is exactly my height and shape--a slender four foot eleven. Mum is a shapely five foot seven. So Xhabbo's twinkling eyes and smiling face and my mother's more cautious face did not exactly line up. However, Xhabbo and I could see eye to eye.

Storytelling with Xhabbo

At dinner, we found out more of Xhabbo's plans, and Mum seemed to genuinely warm up to him. Over the next couple of days, we both felt that there was something very disarming about Xhabbo. There was no craftiness or deceitfulness about him. Even though he was generally quiet and comfortable with silence, when he did speak, it was like you were hearing his thoughts unmodified. And even though Xhabbo sometimes spoke quite slowly, it was not because he was choosing his words as I sometimes did, it was because he was trying to give you exactly the right word in order to be really truthful. As though every word was important and would do something. And he didn't want an ill-chosen word to do something unintended.

I spent a lot of time over the next few days with Xhabbo around the fire. I felt at times like we were in a forest, or savanna, or desert. Maybe it was because his mind was shaped by the Kalahari that he so loved. At times we would come into a silence, like a clearing in the forest, and we'd pick up our drums and drum together and then drift from music back to words and then back to silence as though there were no borders.

When I told the story of my giraffe, Tum, Xhabbo jumped up and started dancing. A little ways into his dance I became aware that it was not Xhabbo in front of the fire but rather a small giraffe, right down to the golden fur and the spots. Maybe it was because his every movement mimicked the posture and attitude of the giraffe so perfectly. I can't quite explain it. My next thought was, *I've seen this before*; it was a moment of déjà vu. There was Tum grabbing the little man's hair off the top of his head. I nearly fell into the fire from surprise and laughter. Maybe this was a common trick of giraffes.

I was so inspired to try dancing a story that I jumped up and started to dance the story of the chimps and the camera. So now it was Xhabbo's turn to nearly fall into the fire laughing. So, through drum, story, silence, laughter, and dance, the story of my Quest was told over the next few nights. Sometimes Mum joined us but often she left us alone. When she was with us, I spoke more through the drum and through dancing.

Mum's Big Fear

I knew Mum was afraid of tigers, as many years before she had seen a friend attacked by a cougar while they were jogging just outside of a place called Canmore in Albert. Now Mum would seem to have an eye for reports and articles about big cats, like cougar and tiger attacks, and would leave them lying around, it would seem, on purpose. I think she wanted to keep me safe by making me more cautious. Maybe she was trying to counterbalance Fa's influence? Mum never told me the details of how her friend was attacked, but I went onto the Web and found the original article in the *Calgary Herald*. It was a big story at the time and was syndicated to many newspapers around the world. There was a good deal of mystery and speculation around why Mum was left unharmed and her friend was killed. I read that a cougar expert had speculated that it might have been because Mum's friend was bleeding at the time and the cougar was attracted to blood. Mum, I'm sure, tried not to hate the cougar, as she loved all living things, but I'm not sure whether she has succeeded yet.

What caught my attention was an interview with the young woman's father a few days after the attack. The father made a plea that residents and others resist the temptation to pressure the Game and Wildlife officials to use this attack as an excuse to trap and kill other cougars that were not involved in the attack. He didn't want to let her death to incite fear or result in punishment of the cougars.

He said that he and his family had moved out of the city to this wild place and that they knew there were risks.

"It was partly because of these risks that we have grown to love this place so fiercely," he said. "Our only daughter was part of the wild beauty of this place; do not kill any cougars for her sake or ours. Leave us to grieve in peace for the one who so recently occupied such a central part in our lives."

So I was careful not to speak of the Tiger King and the quest to warn the Queen of Queens in Mother's presence--and I told Xhabbo why. I could see that Xhabbo was not as good at secrets as I was. So I confess I didn't know if he'd tell Mum, or what would happen when he did.

Xhabbo Agrees to Be Their Guide

After the storytelling festival, it turned out that Xhabbo planned to return to the Kalahari for a while rather than to New York City.

At dinner that night, with Mum present, I asked if we could accompany him to the Kalahari.

"It would be my honour to travel with you both," Xhabbo replied.

So it looked like we were going to Africa over the Christmas holidays after all!

The day finally came, and together we all headed to the airport. Xhabbo insisted that it be the same driver that picked him up from the airport ten days ago.

Where Xhabbo had got a live chicken from I could not even guess. I was worried that Xhabbo was going to make a sacrifice of the chicken on the doorstep of our home, for something like a safe return to Africa. But fortunately, the chicken was for the taxi driver, whom Xhabbo greeted like a long-lost friend. We rode for an hour and a half in a taxi with a chicken who obviously did not like to be travelling inside a car with humans at sixty miles an hour. It was certainly appropriate that our journey began in a way that was out of the ordinary.

CHAPTER FIVE
CAPTAIN MOPANI AND THE GREAT BIRD

Taking to the Air

Upon our arrival at the airport, Xhabbo was filled with a strange mixture of excitement and dread. I was, too, but it appeared to be more extreme for Xhabbo. He said he needed to talk to the pilot before he would fly in the plane.

"Why?" I asked.

"I want to know if the bird we will be travelling on can fly."

Surprised, I blurted out that an airplane is a very big bird, but of course it can fly. Xhabbo reminded me that this is not necessarily correct and started listing off all the large flightless birds that he knew of.

Even though I was pretty uncomfortable, I brought Xhabbo to the counter and tried to explain Xhabbo's concern to the attendant. I was surprised at how helpful she was. She told us we could join the others at early boarding at the door of the "Great Bird." Then on board the plane, she let the flight attendant know we wished to see the pilot. Xhabbo nodded and smiled as though we were making a most reasonable request. Mum, Xhabbo, and I joined the first-class passengers and mothers with young children for early boarding.

At the door of the plane, we asked to see the captain. They took us through to the cockpit of the Great Bird, as I was now starting to call it. The pilot introduced himself to us as Captain Mopani.

"I am Singhalese," he said, "from the kraal of Matabele in the heart of the Kalahari."

My jaw dropped.

"I am Xhabbo, which means 'to dream' in the language of the !Kung

San. We are the First Peoples of the Kalahari. These are my friends of the Tribe of Canadians from the kraal of Mt. Albert," responded Xhabbo.

"Welcome on board the Great Bird," said Captain Mopani.

As if Captain Mopani knew exactly what to say, he continued, "The health of this Great Bird is exceptional. She is young but experienced enough for this long a journey. I have flown ostriches before, and it is no easy thing to get them off the ground and into the air, let alone keep them in the air."

Xhabbo was nodding his head and, with his walking stick, which he would not be parted from, did what he always did when he was in full agreement: he *"smote the ground,"* which made quite a noise and brought the flight attendants running.

But this Captain Mopani took in stride and continued, "In his experience, this particular Great Bird rose from the runway with the strength of a flock of cranes rising like smoke from the surface of Lake Victoria."

With this, Mopani *"smote the ground"* with such force that I thought he'd put a hole in the cockpit floor, but you could see at a glance that all fear had flown from Xhabbo's glowing face.

Aboard the Great Bird

We thanked the captain and were escorted to our seats. That had been very strange, I had to admit, but also, as a result, I had much more confidence in this particular Great Bird and its captain. So we could sit back and better enjoy the flight. During the thunderous takeoff, I imagined being in the midst of thousands of cranes rising up *like smoke* from the surface of Lake Victoria at dusk. Then I slept.

When I awoke, there was nothing but blue . . . blue above, and blue below. Instead of watching in-flight movies, I found Xhabbo's stories much more fascinating. Xhabbo had a flute with him that he played from time to time to punctuate a story or to use to represent a character in the story, like a honey bird.

There was something irregular about the flute, so I asked if I could see it. "What are these markings inside the flute?" I asked.

"They are what's left of the termite tracks," Xhabbo replied. "You do not need to hollow the flute out yourself. Why would I do this when it is what termites naturally do? All our pipes and musical instruments, even the djembe you were given, has been hollowed out by termites. We all work together co-operatively--not just humans, but as many forms of life as we can dream of. I imagine this is what the Garden of Eden that you left was like; some of us First Peoples are still living in our Garden of

Eden, or at least trying to. For the Bushmen, our Eden is the Kalahari."

This was of course why Xhabbo had not laughed at me when I related my conversation with a giraffe or with the bees; for him, it was perfectly natural. I fell asleep again dreaming of termites, and, of all things, a praying mantis. I told Xhabbo about this, and he just gave me a knowing nod.

"This is your captain speaking. My name is Captain Mopani, which in the language of my people means 'osprey.' We are at a cruising altitude of 29,000 feet, just above the migratory altitude of those high flyers, the bar-headed geese. With each international flight, the captain receives a flight route and a manifest. The captain's job is to review satellite weather reports and, based on these, submit a flight plan. Before I submit any flight plan, I overlay it with a three-dimensional map of migratory bird flight paths and alter my flight plans accordingly. It's one way for this Great Bird to look out for smaller birds.

"We are now leaving the South Atlantic Ocean and approaching the shores of Namibia and will be arriving in the capital, Windhoek, in approximately forty-five minutes. The time there is 6:48 p.m., and the current temperature is a sultry eighty-two degrees. I will descend to my minimum allowed ceiling of 12,000 feet so you can enjoy a bird's eye view of the majestic and varied landscape of the Kalahari.

"To one of our passengers, Xhabbo, who is returning to his ancestral home, I would like to extend a special welcome. To each and every one of you I hope you enjoy the remainder of your flight and thank you for travelling Air d'Afrique."

For a few minutes, the passage around our aisle was jammed with colourful and majestic-looking passengers congratulating Xhabbo on his return.

The touchdown was unlike any other landing. Windhoek is perched between two mountain ranges and requires a rapid drop in altitude just before our approach to the runway. So our landing was more like a swoop and then a sudden pulling up, and our touchdown was like a feather fall. There was no feeling of transition between the air and the ground except for the sound of the tires on the tarmac. There were cheers and shouts of "Mopani!" and "Osprey!" up and down the aircraft. Xhabbo had his flute out and had improvised a song of praise for this amazing Great Bird and its pilot while everyone around us was clapping and swaying along.

"Dorothy's not in Kansas anymore," Fa would sometimes say to me. Well, that about summed it up.

Arrival: Windhoek, Namibia, Africa

When we deplaned I did not recognize Windhoek as an airport. It was a modern enough building, but to me, lineups and airports are synonymous--that's a good adult word for similar. Canadians naturally form lines even if there are only two people waiting (Fa was an exception). This does not happen here. Here I am enveloped, surrounded on all sides, immersed, all my senses overwhelmed. You are not a bystander, you are a participant--whether you want to be or not. I wanted to shout, "Step behind the line! Give me some space! I need air--everybody stop moving!" It was tough acclimatizing to Africa.

Interestingly enough, I had found out in my research that bees also have very definite personal space issues. To protect the hive and in a constant struggle to give the hive structural strength, bees will seal any space off with wax and propolis, their sticky household glue made from plant resins. This means that if you want to remove any honey or even to inspect the hive, you had to cut it open; a violence to the hive that disrupted and sometimes destroyed the colony. But this guy named Langstroth from Massachusetts with what was kindly referred to at the time as "head troubles" became obsessed with bees. On October 31, 1851, Lorenzo Langstroth discovered that bees would not seal off any space less than one-eighth of an inch. This discovery applied to beekeeping was the grail. It meant that you could design a hive with removable chambers that stored the honey, called supers, as long as the space between them was less than one-eighth of an inch. On realizing the significance of his discovery, he ran through the streets shouting "Eureka!"

Namibia is called "the land of contrasts," "the land God made in anger," "the ageless land." It is also the second-most sparsely populated country in the world, after Mongolia. And although Namibia has seven national languages and twenty-one language groups, its official language is English. Namibia's currency is the Namibian dollar, which is on par with the South African *rand*, which is also accepted as currency.

As we made our way through the old town, it felt like an accident was going to happen in every moment. The chickens and the wandering dogs, the shopkeepers who come out of the stores to lure you in, the beggars who leaned over you, the cab drivers opening their doors as you came by, the occasional ostrich being chased by someone, the little children weaving in and out of everything that moves--including your own legs, and in every other square inch of space, a bicycle on the move. There were constant exceptions to the concept of lanes. Every moment looked like the moment before an accident, but somehow everything just missed each other and continued on going. Don't believe the pictures in the Windhoek, Namibia brochures and websites; they are at a level of deception that even Fa would have frowned upon. From the brochures, you'd have thought you were going to a quaint little village in the Bavarian Alps.

Mum and I didn't have much money--the airfare had been a stretch for us--so Xhabbo was able to convince us to take the bus to Himba, the village near where uLangalibalela, the Great Witch Doctor, lived. It would be a journey of many days, taking us across borders and into the vast region, spanning four countries, known as the Kalahari.

CHAPTER SIX
UUKULE AND THE ROAD TO HIMBA

The Great Wallow

If I thought that the airport was wild, there was nothing that could prepare me for the bus terminal. There had been a deluge of rain overnight and the bus terminal was simply a farm field with no drainage and no pavement anywhere in sight. It was like a gigantic wallow. The buses had aptly transformed themselves into Hippos. Hippos that were revving up, rocking back and forth, spewing black smoke, fishtailing and sending up plumes of oil-laden mud onto anyone who managed to avoid being run down.

None of the buses were lined up and there was no sign on them saying where they were headed. There was no board showing bus arrivals and departures, there was no obvious way to pay and get a ticket. It was utterly disorienting, my mum looked as surprised as I felt. However, Xhabbo looked totally unconcerned, even happy. He led us to the outer perimeter of the field to where a large crowd was gathered. He picked me up and put me on his shoulders and I could see that the crowed fanned out from what looked more like a hot-dog vendor than ticket agent.

Twenty or thirty buses all descending into the area and attempting to leave, and the only employee looked to be a hot-dog vendor. Xhabbo gave me some money and told me to wave it in the air. A few moments later the hot-dog vendor/ticket agent pointed across the crowd toward me. Xhabbo told me to hand the fifty-*rand* note forward and he mentioned Himba, the name of the village we were travelling to. Above that vast crowd, our money travelled from one hand to the other along with the name of the village. Then it was like the wave of hands in reverse as our change came back with three bus tickets that had obviously made the trip to Himba several times before.

Moses, Our Guide across the Great Wallow

There were young boys agilely darting between the buses like tugboats with passengers in tow. Somehow they knew which bus was going where, and it was obviously not safe to head into the wallow without one of these young boys as a guide. Quick as a flash, once we had our tickets, a small boy appeared out of the mud and took my hand and led us into the wallow of rollicking hippos. He took us through at a breakneck pace with my mum right behind and Xhabbo pulling up the rear. We circled, veered left and right, pirouetted, dashed, jumped over, screeched to a halt . . . we even once entered a bus, walked down the aisle, and exited out the back. Finally, we came to a bus near the middle of the wallow that was covered in mud from top to bottom. Passengers had cleared small holes in the mud so they could see out their windows, and the front windshield wipers were going full blast to keep a small section relatively clear.

The young boy climbed up on top of the bus and placed our bags on a large luggage rack. Then he came down and ushered us onto the bus, which was already more than full. People had settled down in the aisles and brought their own stools. The young boy started shuffling people around on the bus, each of whom appeared reluctant, but willing enough to follow his directions. Just behind the driver, there were five or six folding chairs set up. The young boy moved three people elsewhere and got us to sit down. We could not move our feet an inch, but supposedly we had prime seats. We handed the young boy, whose name was, appropriately, Moses, a few *rand*. Moses said he'd wait on top of the bus to watch our luggage until the bus left. I later found out that "Moses" is the fifth most common name for boys in Namibia.

He introduced me to another boy who was about my age: Uukule, who was the bus driver's assistant. Our hippo started to show signs of waking up. The door closed, it belched black smoke and started rocking back and forth, and moments later, we were charging through the wallow, swinging this way and that as we avoided both getting stuck and colliding with other buses. Through the little smudged clearing in the window, I could see people jumping out of our way. Finally, we lurched up from the wallow and out onto the dusty road that would take us toward the Great Witch Doctor known as uLangalibalela.

Atop the Bus

Day melts into night in the vast landscape of the Kalahari. Red dust is everywhere. We get to stretch our legs and take a rest stop wherever along the road the bus breaks down. The driver and Uukule climb underneath. Uukule appears from time to time to retrieve a well-used spare part or tool from the back of the bus. Every so often, some offending part is brought out from under the bus, and a group gathers around and makes clucking sounds of disapproval. Everything moves in slow motion as though we have been placed in suspended animation for the long trip. We get back in, sometimes stopping for food in a small village where the locals sell delicious fried plantain, cornbread, and couscous. Fortunately, I don't eat meat because there is no easy way to tell the difference between goat and what they call bush rat. Then off we go again, through another day and night. Occasionally we see animals in the distance, but nothing up close.

On day two, Uukule comes over to tell me that as we are far enough from the capital, I can ride up on the roof with the luggage if I want to. I ask Mum right away, and she is not keen on the idea. After a few minutes, Xhabbo suggests that perhaps we could all go up there on the roof of the bus together. I start to jump up and down, and Mum relents. I cannot wait. At the next stop, Uukule leads all of us onto the top of the bus, where we find comfortable spots in between the luggage. The ride from that point on is fabulous. There are few things as exceptional as a 360-degree view of the Kalahari. At dusk, we pass through an orchard of night-blooming jasmine, and my eyes roll back in ecstasy when I catch a glimpse of the huge African sun dipping below the horizon . . . the heat rising from the ground creating ripple-like distortions.

Ray Doubts Her Quest

While I lay there on top of the bus, the sound of the wind was too loud for any of us to talk for long. So I dozed and had time for thoughts. Doubts started to creep in. Was I imagining things? In this massive land, in which I was just a speck, was there actually a hidden war going on between Kings and Bees and Giraffes and Tigers that would determine the fate of the world? And what could an eleven-year-old girl from Canada--Mt. Albert, of all places--have to do with something this big, even if any of it were true? Thoughts like this grew, as did the discomfort of knowing that I had deceived Mum. Maybe I could just forget the Quest and enjoy the holiday, talk to the Witch Doctor only about Fa, and then the deception would just kind of evaporate. Hmmm.

The farther we got from people, the more wildlife we saw. Ostriches ran alongside the bus at the same speed as us before veering off. I think they were drafting us, using the bus to break the wind as they travelled across the endless plains or veldt. We saw hippos by the river, lots of zebras, and herds of elephants all in a row with their trunks wrapped around the tail of the elephant in front like a group of preschoolers on an outing. I will always appreciate my experiences at the zoo, but seeing these magnificent animals in their wild habitat gives you a feeling of vastness--in the vastness of the whole.

Through all of this, the bus continued on through the smaller and smaller villages--or kraals, as Uukule called them. We created some shade up top out of the luggage, and I crawled under and slept. I was woken by Xhabbo, who was pointing to something in the distance. I couldn't quite make it out; it was a herd of something--wild giraffes, Xhabbo stated. My heart leapt. This was one of the moments I'd been waiting for.

Encounter with the Wild Giraffes

It looked like the giraffes were headed toward us and were travelling at approximately the same speed, which was fifty miles per hour. Half an hour later, they were only a mile away and growing much larger. It looked like they were making a beeline right across where the bus was headed. Thirty seconds later, they were only half a mile away on a direct intercept course. Surely the bus driver must see them; or perhaps on the large, open plains, where there was no precise road, he had fallen asleep. Everyone on top was at full attention, I started to cry out, and Uukule started to bang on top of the bus.

Then, just fifty feet ahead, the herd passed in front of the bus. Was the bus driver playing "chicken" with herd of giraffes, or did he just fall asleep? The sound was incredible; it was like standing on the platform as a high-speed GO train passed by. The bus bounced on the shaking earth. Surely the driver was awake, now! As we passed in the wake of their stampede, we could not see anything in the whirlwind of dust. Then, in the midst of the dust, right beside me, appeared the head of a giraffe, and clear as a bell I heard my name--"Ray"--and it was gone. Moments later, the dust storm passed, and the herd could be seen moving off into the distance, with one giraffe trailing slightly behind. When I asked, nobody had heard my name being called out, but Uukule said he was just able to make out a giraffe's head above the bus, or so he thought.

Out ahead was a small kraal, but as we got closer, we could see a large, manned gate and a fence that stretched out toward the horizon in both directions. A bright new sign said, "Welcome to Kgalagadi Transfrontier

Park." I had read about it on the Web and picked up a brochure for the newly formed park in Windhoek. The brochure stated that:
Kgalagadi means "place of thirst" in the San language. The Kgalagadi Transfrontier Park is a newly formed park, with little or no human presence. It is a place where the red dunes and scrub fade into infinity and herds of gemsbok, springbok, eland, and blue wildebeest follow the seasons, where imposing camel thorn and baobab trees provide shade for huge black-maned lions and vantage points for leopards, tigers, and many raptors. The Kgalagadi Transfrontier National Park--previously the Kalahari National Park--was proclaimed in 1931 mainly to protect the migrating game. Together with the adjacent Gemsbok National Park in Botswana, the Kgalagadi Transfrontier Park spans four countries and comprises an area of over 3.6 million hectares--one of very few conservation areas of this magnitude left in the world.

The Standoff

The bus stopped before we entered the border town, and we climbed off the roof of the bus. The bus was nearly empty now. I asked Uukule what had happened to everybody.
"There are less and less people living out here," was his reply.
"Why?" I asked.
"I can't speak about it now. I'll tell you more when we pass the checkpoint and after we enter the park."
I was excited to be entering the park, but I sensed something was not right. At the gate there was trouble. The guard was not going to allow Xhabbo to enter the park. The bus driver confronted the guard, who stood his ground and told him to back away as he swung his rifle from his back into his hands.
Now my mum stepped forward, and with an air of authority, said, "We're not proceeding without our guide. He travelled with us from Canada, and we are not leaving without him."
It was a tense standoff. In the intervening silence, nothing moved. I walked over and put my hand in Xhabbos. More silence. Uukule came over and he held my hand, then my Mother joined us and we just stood there in front of the guard with the rifle.
Now I know what a standoff is. We didn't glare at the guard, we just looked down at the earth and stood there holding hands. I felt a tremendous surge of some kind of energy through our hands; it was a connection and a kind of power. I'm sure it made each of us glow like light bulbs. I think the guard saw this and realized that he would not win, and so he backed down.

"Go!" he said. We wasted no time getting back into the bus in case he changed his mind.

Over the next few minutes, Xhabbo pointed out the phrase in the brochure that stated that the newly formed Kgalagadi Transfrontier National Park had little or no human presence.

Incredulous, I said, "Surely this does not include the Bushmen of the Kalahari--the San Peoples!"

"Yes," Uukule stated. "They are being relocated outside the park."

I had read on Wikipedia that the Bushmen/San ancestors predated the genetic changes within the rest of the human population, making them a "genetic Adam" from which all humans can ultimately trace their genetic heritage. Now they were being moved off land that belonged to them and to which they had belonged since the very beginning of human time. It was a final thrust into the heart of the First of the First peoples. I looked over and saw tears in Xhabbo's eyes. I was crying, too, and wrapped my arms around him.

Arrival at the End of the Road

It was not long before the light and joy came back to Xhabbo's face and he began dancing up and down inside the bus. Up ahead was a Bushman kraal. It was made up of small, domed, mud structures that formed a circle. I had seen that pattern many times before. As we got closer, I cried out, "Yes! It's a hive. The kraal is the shape of a hive."

"Yes," cried out Xhabbo, "exactly! We know ourselves as the people of the honey. In New York City, I gravitated to math and geometry. One of the things I studied was the honeycomb structure, which is a trihedral pyramidal shape, which means that it is composed of three rhombi. This is the shape used by the honeybee and is the ideal geometry for a three-dimensional structure. These shapes naturally occur on the boundaries of soap bubbles."

From the village we can hear singing. The bus stops just outside the kraal and we remain quiet until the end of the song. Xhabbo translates the words of the traditional song:

The people beat the drum, so that the bees may become abundant for the people. And the people carry honey. And the people bring the honey home. And the people take honey to the women at home. For the women are hungry for honey. Therefore, the men take honey to the women at home; for they wish that the women may make a drum for them, so that they may dance, when the women are satisfied with honey. For the women do not dance and frolic when they are hungry.

At the end of the song, there is clapping and laughter. The few of us left on the bus walk the quarter mile into the village. Xhabbo is welcomed like a long-lost brother. The bus driver's family lives here at the end of the road. He will stay a few nights before the long journey back to Windhoek. A big fuss is made of Mum and me; the girls all want to touch my hair. Most can speak some English and they are finding names for me: Little Lioness and Bee, because of my strawberry-blonde hair.

There is much celebrating. The drum signals the group back to the circle for more dancing and singing. There is no way not to participate--non-participation is not an option. You are brought in no matter what, no wallflowers, here. The elderly still dance, sing, drum, stomp their feet, or just stamp their walking sticks and clap! Children are everywhere playing and joining in.

Finally, when I can no longer stand up for one more dance, the children shout, "Xhabbo, Xhabbo, tell us a story!" Then the elders chime in and so does everyone. People gather around Xhabbo, a hush falls, and you can hear the sounds of the bush around the village. It is the Kalahari at night. There can be no more perfect backdrop to a story. Xhabbo waits as though the land tells the first part of the story. Then he begins: "In the place of white rain, rain that falls slowly to the ground and stays for seven cycles of the moon . . . in a place where people build caves in the air and everyone travels at the speed of a cheetah . . . In that place, we walked down a tunnel toward the Great Silver Bird. We spoke with the one who guides it and he told us that the bird was in good health and not like the Great White Flightless One."

Everyone broke out into roars of laughter at this. One person jumped up and mimicked the ostrich, transforming himself as if every bone and joint moved like an ostrich that was trying to fly. More laughter . . . others joined the dancer, and you could see people travelling down tunnels and climbing into caves in the sky. Once everyone settled down again, the story continued well into the night, which included all of us holding hands in front of the guard, right up to the present moment.

Mum was asked to tell a story and she looked over at me for help. I felt something strongly in common with how the Bushmen saw the world and how everything spoke to them. So I was less afraid to speak now than I was to speak in front of my class. I told the story of the giraffe and the little man. I had a camera with me so I could demonstrate the story. When I came to the moment where the little man loses his hair, there was silence. I looked at each of them, a little boy giggled but everyone else looked sad. I later found out that it was a terrible thing for anyone to lose his hair; he would get burnt by the sun. It was the first of many times that I would suddenly be reminded that the Bushmen do not laugh at others' misfortune.

CHAPTER SEVEN
ULANGALIBALELA:
A SOUL NOT SEPARATE FROM THE LAND

Ray Shares the Story of Her Quest

Even though they did not laugh, they seemed to enjoy the story and wanted another. So I tried the story told to me by the bee. You could not hear a pin drop except where the story was punctuated by the sounds of the night. I ended with how the Dark King Mobutu sent out the tigers to hunt for the First Hive. In the distance, you could hear the roar of a lion. I looked up and everyone was nodding their heads with tears in their eyes. After a while there were whispers, and then a child spoke: "Tell us the ending." They all joined in, "Tell us the ending!" The elders smote the ground with their walking sticks. Some of the children started to cry out loud.

"I don't know the end of the story," I cried out.

Xhabbo jumped in. "Little Sun has travelled all the way from the Land where Water Stands Still to discover the end of this story."

A hush fell upon the group.

An elder finally spoke, "Little Sun, Bee Girl with the Mane of a Lion, we are here to help you on your journey. Ask and we shall give it to you if it is in our power. Your Quest is our Quest."

Everyone looked very serious and was nodding their heads in agreement--except Mum; she had a very surprised look on her face indeed. As the sun was starting to rise, we all quickly headed to bed for a few hours.

On Our Way to the Great Witch Doctor

The mud huts have a remarkable ability to stay cool right into the heat of the day. By the time I woke up, it was noon, and the entire village was preparing for our journey to the great uLangalibalela, who lived up on the plateau. His name around the village was spoken with a hush. Mum came over and told me that I had become quite a remarkable storyteller and that last story was a real doozy.

"Where did you hear that one?" she asked.

Fortunately, she didn't wait for an answer.

"Well wherever you got that one from, you should tell them the truth of why you came here: to ask uLangalibalela about Fa."

We were interrupted, and so the conversation ended there for the moment.

By late afternoon, everything was ready for our journey, and we set out across plains that have stood still in time. All the large boulders and big trees have names that express the spirit and history of the place. Places like: Twee Rivieren, Mata Mata, Bitterpan, Kieliekrankie, Urikaruus, Gharagab, Kij Kij, Kamqua. All with a story that stretches back so far in time that some of the stories tell of the time before stories. We pass by rocks on which their direct ancestors had painted what was important to them. Xhabbo traced his fingers over this stone with its ancient drawings and symbols and said, "I don't have a soul that is separate from this stone, from this land. Without you and your mother, I would not have been able to return here."

Sometimes I closed my eyes and then opened them. Every moment, I was looking out on a picture-perfect painting or a splendid scene from a movie. Always ever-changing and yet constantly perfect. We just had to put the camera away, because there were no bad shots. The Bushmen had such magnificent faces; the old ones had such wild lines, each with big, big grins for me. The children were beautiful and full of curiosity. The young girls were at first shy around me but soon became friends; and the men were funny and full of emotion. Every person took a great photograph and they belonged completely to the landscape that we moved through.

The hunters caught small game, and we ate what the boys and girls had foraged and snared, along with some greens that were collected on the way. I found that they had planted many tubers along the paths to places they regularly travelled to. "Roadside root vegetables," I called them. These were delicious baked in the fire at night and served with couscous and flatbread. At night, Mum and I slept in a tent we had brought with us, and the fourteen Bushmen who were accompanying us on the journey slept in the open on reed mats in a circle around us. We lay there listening to the frequent, screams, shrieks, squeals, roars, howls, laughs, cries, whistles, thumps, croaks, clicks, cracks, booms, and whoops throughout the night. I could see that Mum was disturbed by the roars most of all. But as there was no jungle with snakes hanging from the trees, I felt safe in the centre of the circle.

Preparing to Meet the Great uLangalibalela

Xhabbo started to teach Mum and me the protocol for meeting the Great uLangalibalela.

I said, "Can't we just play it by ear?"

Xhabbo looked horrified, like he'd seen a ghost. Maybe that's how people became a ghost? To please Xhabbo, I agreed to follow the protocol.

First Xhabbo said, "It's wrong to think of uLangalibalela as just a healer of the body. He could read a person's shadow and heal those who were 'thin' in heart and mind. uLangalibalela has been born into a land of dreams and he can interpret and travel into them. As his power grows, he is able also see over the 'rim of the years.' He is the greatest in all the land, and as a result, a small village of people are drawn to him, mostly women, as they are better able to recognize these hidden powers.

"First," Xhabbo continued, "we must not go straight to uLangalibalela's hut. We must wait to be summoned. And it is best if we do not even use one of uLangalibalela's trees for shade. Do not presume anything and do not take anything; to do so would be to show disrespect. How well you show respect is one of the ways uLangalibalela sees who you are. This extends right down to the smallest gestures and actions. The other place that the Great uLangalibalela sees is straight into the heart. He can see into the heart at a great distance, even now he may be looking. If we either show disrespect to him or the land, or we are thin of heart, he will not see us. That is the worst thing that can happen. He will say, 'I cannot see you.' In this case, we must return, and the journey is for nothing. If he says, 'I cannot see you well,' then we reply that we have brought gifts to help him see us better. That is why the goats are travelling with us. You and your mum should think of a gift to offer.

"If, however, he says, 'I have seen you,' or, 'I have seen you since a certain time or place,' this is best, as he is already at the heart of the matter. If this is the case, we bring in the gifts immediately."

"Is that all?" I asked just a bit sarcastically.

"No," Xhabbo replied. "That is the bare minimum; there many other protocols."

"I don't think they will be necessary," I said.

"They may be," Xhabbo replied; "but I will advise you on these as we go along."

To be honest, I was a bit confused as to how to behave. Fa had said don't bow down to any person; and yet was this simply a "person," or was uLangalibalela something more?

Our final few miles was up a long ascent to a plateau that was considerably higher than the surrounding land. The vegetation became lush and it was becoming more and more like a garden as we went higher. We came across women who were singing as they worked. What a rhythm they created as they hoed the ground together in unison, what power and fluid motion they put into tending the land! Why have we stopped singing together as we work? I wondered. Maybe we have stopped really working together? That's why we need all this teambuilding and leadership training. How the singing and rhythm seemed to elevate what they were doing and turn it into creative work! They did not even stop as we passed by. My mother and I were used to drawing attention in this part of the world, but these women seemed totally focused on what they were doing at that moment.

There was no question that uLangalibalela's kraal was the village of a great man. There was no question of its being a hive; and from every point around the village, you could see 360 degrees to the horizon, from sunrise to sunset. You could see in the distance dust stirred up like smoke coming off the plains and if you looked more closely, you saw herds of giraffes, elephants, or even rhinos on the move. You could see anyone approaching from a great distance away. You could see little pockets of weather and big storms arrive and depart. But the question still remained: could uLangalibalela see into hidden things like the location of the Hive of Hives? Or the human heart? And could he see into tomorrow? I was very curious to find out.

It began to rain. I had not seen any rain since we arrived in Africa, but according to Xhabbo, up here it was not that unusual, being so lush.

"uLangalibalela can control the weather," Xhabbo stated.

Well, really I'd had quite enough of what uLangalibalela was supposed to be able to do. "I suppose he can part the Red Sea as well," I said.

With no sarcasm, Xhabbo replied, "From whom do you think Moses learned how to do it?"

I had to admit that was the most plausible explanation I'd yet heard so far.

"This is a good omen," Xhabbo went on to say.

"A good omen? We're soaked to the bone and standing here in our wet clothes!"

What I didn't yet realize was that rain is never a curse in this part of the world; it's always a blessing. Water is the most respected of all the elements. Precious beyond measure, all life here depends on it and is regularly lost without it. I come from a place where there is such an abundance of fresh water that we have squandered, polluted, and devalued it. I made a promise to myself that I would try to see water the way Xhabbo and the Bushmen saw it before I returned to the place where water stands still.

Meeting the Witch Doctor

Really, it's a lot of fun to get totally soaked when its warm out, and you haven't washed in a week. Before long, a young boy came to us and told us that uLangalibalela had summoned us. We came into the large, covered space at the centre of the kraal. Light shone in through many openings, and it was very clean, orderly, and somewhat sparse, which surprised me. The rain drummed on the roof as we waited for the Great Witch Doctor. When he came in, Xhabbo stood up, so each of us followed suit and stood up. uLangalibalela was a very beautiful man, taller than most of the Bushmen, with some white hair and the simplest of white cotton cloaks. He carried a long staff with some amazing carvings on it. It was like a scene from *Lord of the Rings*, except he looked like a healthier African version of Gandalf.

uLangalibalela sat down and beckoned us to do so. Right away, he spoke of knowing Fa. This was a little surprising, as there would have been no one to arrive before us and tell him. Maybe he saw the resemblance, though.

After a few moments, he said, "I have heard he has a daughter."

"Yes, I'm the daughter!" I called out.

"I hear you but I cannot see you, little one."

"But I'm right here!" I shouted.

"I can hear you, but I cannot see you," uLangalibalela repeated.

I was shocked and looked over at Xhabbo pleadingly. Xhabbo was unsure but asked how many did the Great uLangalibalela see?

"I can see two," the Witch Doctor replied as he stood up and walked out.

I felt embarrassed and very upset. I went over to Mum and cried. Xhabbo looked very sad and uncertain. I came over and hugged him as well.

"Why do you think he can't see me?"

I think Xhabbo knew but would not say.

"What do we do next?" I asked.

"Well," said Xhabbo, "this is highly unusual--that he can hear a person but not see them. It would seem to indicate that there is hope that he will hear *and* see you if the conditions are right. There is a jungle a day's walk from here. It is a somewhat dangerous place, where snakes hang from the trees."

This I did not want to hear.

"Maybe we should go back," I said.

"No," Mum stated.

I looked startled, "What about the danger?"

"Fa would never have let us turn back here," Mum said.

"That's fine for you to say--the great Witch Doctor saw you."

Xhabbo reminded me not to take this personally, "It is for your own good that uLangalibalela has not seen you."

"It doesn't feel good to me," I replied.

But as I thought more about it I remembered that in the past my discomfort was sometimes just my own conscience poking me. Mum would always point it out to me, so I was starting to be able to recognize the sharp poke of conscience.

"Ok," I cried out, "jungle with snakes it is, then!"

"I need to stay here," Mum said.

"Well that's convenient, given that there are no tigers or other big cats around here!"

I immediately regretted saying it. Mum just hugged me.

CHAPTER EIGHT
MUM CONFRONTS HERE OWN FEARS

The Real Wallow

It was just Xhabbo and I who headed down from the plateau toward the Jungle. I would have felt safer being together with the fourteen other Bushmen we had travelled here with. But I also felt that Xhabbo would not have suggested we go to the jungle if it was really that dangerous. We began to circle a large wetlands that many animals used as a wallow. The flocks were too numerous to even guess at. There were storks, cranes, herons, and egrets of so many colours. One reason for such large gatherings of animals and birds is the great distance between bodies of water. I had heard that nowhere on earth are there such vast flocks of water birds and flamingos; the Kalahari has the greatest gatherings of flamingos. I saw the entire sky filled with flamingos as they leapt up into the air in one great burst of pink. We saw masses of cranes doing an extraordinary mating dance. It was like watching a wild ballet. Xhabbo told me that dying Bushmen look back on their life as though it were the dance of a crane. What a beautiful way to look back on your life, I thought. I decided to remember this. I had of course already worked out my last words.

"Blood! Isn't this stuff supposed to be on the *inside?*" was what I had planned to say.

This seemed trivial in comparison, but I told Xhabbo anyway, forgetting yet again that Bushmen don't laugh at others' misfortune.

It was like animal rush hour. We had to be careful, as we two humans were amongst the smallest of the creatures at this vast watering hole.

Entering the Jungle

On the other side of the lake, we followed the river into a valley where the vegetation grew more and more dense. Soon we were in the jungle. One way to know is that the sounds get more intense and it gets harder and harder to move ahead.

"Why don't you have a machete to cut through the jungle?" I asked Xhabbo.

"Bushmen don't use machetes."

Xhabbo led me to a small clearing where we sat down and ate some of the flatbread and couscous.

"There are protocols to every place you go; know the protocols and you prosper and remain safe. Ignore them, and your journey will be unnecessarily hard and perilous."

That made me remember a time Fa and I went canoeing in a place called Algonquin. It rained on each of the seven days. Not all day, but each day. Fa and I moved in the sunny periods, slept during the rain, avoided the long, muddiest portages, and kept warm by using standing dead wood for our fires. We had a great time. Two young men did pretty much the opposite and just stayed with what they had planned to do despite the weather. They didn't know how to find dry wood and went through the longest, muddiest portages in the park. At the take-out point, they were a mass of insect bites, covered in mud, hadn't had hot food in days, and were sleep deprived. They told us about their ordeal.

After my experience with uLangalibalela I was more receptive to knowing the protocols.

"What are the protocols for this place?" I asked eagerly.

"There are many specific ones for the jungle, and if you watch what I do, you will learn some of them. However, there are some general ones that apply everywhere.

"All living things experience three general states: *Curiosity, Fear, and Hunger.* You must be able to recognize each of these states within yourself and in other living things. This is why we seek to observe everything around us, to determine these states, to know the others' true motivation. Then we respond according to what we've observed, which is based on what is really happening, not some preprogrammed response. We become good at communicating our response as clearly as we can in order to avoid misunderstanding. To any animal or other living thing that is Curious, we respond with Playfulness. To another animal or living thing that is Fearful, we respond with Docility. To an animal or living thing that is Hungry, we share our food, or, if they see us as food we make ourselves Fierce and appear bigger or stronger than our adversary in order to avoid conflict. These are the general protocols. I believe they are the same for every ecosystem, including your Algonquin. Observe them and you'll stay safe; become skilled at them and you'll move through the world like a stone through water."

"Why don't you use a machete to clear a path through the jungle?" I asked.

"We like to travel lightly and quietly and not leave a swath of unnecessary destruction behind us. Bushmen are also very careful not to create fear by being a threat and therefore provoke an unnecessary fight. Too many in the West do not observe this rule. Every living thing has a threat radius and a lethal capability. Animals with a big threat radius are obviously more dangerous, as are animals that are more lethal. Tigers and leopards are deadly, as they have both a large threat radius and a high lethal capability.

"A snake, for instance," I was all ears by now; "snakes have on the other hand a very small threat radius and high lethal capability. Their very small threat radius makes them quite safe. They will not strike unless you step on them or cut the branch that they are on. Of course, this takes a high degree of awareness both to look where you're going and where you're placing each foot.

"We follow a process of zooming in on the small and zooming out to the larger picture. We learn this as children, and it becomes part of our nature. We do not carelessly walk and talk, like we are taking a stroll in Central Park--well, that's probably not a good example. Central Park is very much like this place. Instead, we listen, observe, and use all our senses to pass through this place safely. Are you willing to try this?"

"If you think I'm ready, Xhabbo."

"Yes, you're good at listening and observing; otherwise I would not have brought you here."

"Do you think it will help uLangalibalela to see me?"

"I don't know, Ray Sun, but it might."

Ray Meets the Big Cat

We spent the next five hours moving quietly through the jungle, over, under, around, but never straight through. We saw many big and small things but we were careful not to provoke.

At one point, Xhabbo said, "Be very still, little one . . . turn now and link arms with me." When I turned around, there, in the trees thirty feet away, I saw a large leopard.

"Now smite the ground hard with your walking stick!"

Which I readily did! We kept our arms linked. In his other hand Xhabbo stood ready with his spear. I glared right into the eyes of the big cat. Another tense standoff! Finally the big cat looked away, turned, and leaped from the tree, disappearing into the jungle in one fluid motion. My heart was beating so loudly I'm sure everything in the forest could hear it.

"You stood firm, Ray Sun," Xhabbo cried out with pride in his voice. "You smote the ground very well, and the tiger spoke to you through its eyes."

Xhabbo told me that we were done here and that it was now time to return to the Great uLangalibalela. As we passed the big wallow, we still needed to walk with caution. We saw a leopard that had fallen prey to something else. The buzzards were moving in. Whatever preyed on a leopard is not something I want to meet. I followed Xhabbo close to the leopard's body. Quick as a flash, Xhabbo took a small section of skin, a tooth, and a claw. Then we moved away swiftly, not wanting to see what showed up next. We left the large watering hole behind and started to climb toward the plateau. Finally, we could slow down and let our minds spread out. While we were walking up the trail, I started to think on what the leopard had said to me through its eyes. I had sensed it was saying something but my heart was beating so hard that I couldn't hear anything else. But I could now understand what it said and I gasped. I burst out, "That leopard told me Mum is in danger!"

"Did it say how, Ray Sun?"

"No, all I know is that we must hurry!"

Mum's Fever

Just then Uukule came down from the Plateau to tell us to hurry, as Mum had come down with a fever after we'd left and was very sick. Soon we were at Mum's side. It was very frightening to see her like this so far from Mt. Albert. This was all my fault. It was my deception that brought us here. Then I realized that there was no time for this kind of thinking. I got to work collecting water and constantly bathing Mum with a cloth to keep her cool. Mum at times was burning hot and was throwing off the furs and at other times was shivering cold, delirious, sometimes babbling and sometimes crying out. It became clear that she was battling something. In the very corner of the room sat uLangalibalela, not moving the entire time. He was like a shadow in the room, there and not there. It was somehow very reassuring having him there, though, even though he appeared to be doing nothing. Time passed; I fell asleep from exhaustion.

Xhabbo and others had collected herbs like feverfew to bring down the fever.

Two days later, Mum seemed to be more comfortable. She smiled and thanked me and then slept the whole night. In the morning, Mum was back. She drank lots of goat's broth and a mixture of herbs for strength. In the night, uLangalibalela had slipped out of the room. During that entire time he had not spoken and only had a specially prepared tea brought to him. Now I slept for the entire day knowing that Mum was ok. That evening, Mum and I sat alone together. It was a cool night and we had a small fire going in the fireplace that was built into the clay wall of the large, domed room that we had to ourselves. We sat in front of the fire wrapped together in skins.

"Mum, I lied to you about why I wanted to come to Africa."

"I know dear. Xhabbo told me that you are on a Quest, but not what it was. He said this must come from you. Although I feel that in some way your reason for not telling me was because of my fear of big cats."

What a relief it was for me to tell the truth, "the whole truth and nothing but the truth," and have my Mum understand. Like a big backpack that you had gotten so used to carrying that only when you finally took it off, did you realize what a burden it had been to carry.

We just sat there in silence for a while, wrapped in love and appreciation of each other.

Fear is Like Poison

"Do you remember anything of what happened in your fever?" I asked Mum.

"Yes, I remember quite a bit. It was more like a powerful experience rather than an illness. There's no doubt I had a fever, but it seemed to be an encounter with fate, or whatever you want to call it. When my friend Pachine was killed by the mountain lion, I felt anger, but hiding behind the anger was guilt. It was guilt and shame that were pursuing me. I was so afraid in the moment of the attack that I could not help her. I just wanted to disappear and so I ran away. So many times in my dreams, I returned to that moment: Each time, I ran away; and each time I ran away, the fear grew. Fear is like poison: It often goes unnoticed in small doses, but over time it gets more powerful until it eventually kills you from the inside. This fever was like the poison of fear coming out of me."

Mum continued, "Somehow I know you met a leopard in the jungle."

"How do you know this? Did Xhabbo tell you?"

"I'm not sure how I know, but in my fever, a tiger was stalking me. I couldn't shake it. I now know what it is like to be hunted--it's both exciting and terrifying. I ran and ran and there was no way it was going to give up; it was terribly hungry and I was no more than a meal to it. The tiger didn't know and didn't care how much I loved you; that was the terrible thing. Why it had not killed me yet I could not understand. There was no way for me to defeat it alone, so at some point in my fever, I realized that I must not be alone.

"That's when I started to see uLangalibalela. Not as himself, but as many of the other animals in the jungle. None of them could singlehandedly defeat the tiger, but each of them together was able to distract, annoy, and delay it. Still, I was getting weaker and weaker, and at my darkest moment I stopped running and finally turned to face the tiger. That's when the leopard appeared; this leopard knew of my love for you and stood at my side. This is how I know you had met a leopard on your journey with Xhabbo. This gave me the courage to take a step toward the hungry tiger; and each step I took, the tiger grew smaller until I was standing right in front of it. It was now the size of a house cat, so I leaned down and ever so carefully let it sniff me and began to stroke it. It purred. 'Let's get you some food,' I said. I turned to the leopard that was beside me and it was gone; in its stead, you were there. I knew everything would be okay at that point, and my fear, guilt, self-doubt, and shame were gone. Now I just felt compassion for myself and Pachine's family."

I told Mum about the interview with Pachine's father.

"That's so beautiful," Mum said. "Thank you for that. It's how I feel now. It just took me longer to get there."

Ray Comes Clean

"Tell me about your Quest, dear."

So I told Mum about the bees and the First Hive, about the Dark King and his army of tigers and how the propagation of life was at stake. I told her of the giraffe's gift and the ability to listen to animals and even bees, and how we must find the First Hive and warn the Queen of Queens.

At the end of it she said, "If it can be done, we will do it, and we will face the danger together."

The next morning, we were summoned by the Great uLangalibalela. As Mum and I were getting ready, Xhabbo arrived with a pair of my jeans. He had patched the holes in them with small pieces of leopard skin and he had made a necklace with the tooth and claw of the leopard. I wriggled into them like they were my own skin and put the necklace on. Mum was beaming at me. The three of us went to meet uLangalibalela.

CHAPTER NINE
TULILIKI:
OUR GUIDE THROUGH THE KALAHARI

uLangalibalela Introduces us to Tuliliki

His first words, once we were seated were, "I have seen each of you for many days now."

Xhabbo whispered in my ear, "This means that he is now at the heart of the matter."

"Each of you has been on a journey that has purified and readied you for what is to come. So let us now speak only of the Quest, of preparing for your journey to the First Hive. There must be no men with you on this journey to the Queen of Queens. We will send most of the Bushmen that accompanied you here back to their villages with gifts from our weavers and gardeners. You will travel with the strongest and most able women from this kraal. One of the women is a honey dreamer and she knows the songs of each of the fifteen species of birds known as honey guides. These birds will assist you on your journey to the First Hive. Her name is Tuliliki."

"What about Xhabbo?" I asked.

"Xhabbo will stay here. I need his help from here in keeping you safe on your journey."

Tuliliki was not what you'd expect. Most of the women here are very handsome and strong with fine voices and colourful clothing. Tuliliki is very tall and slender, which is not common in this part of Africa. Xhabbo told me that hundreds of years ago, a hunting party from up north in the area that is now called Burundi travelled down to the Kalahari and settled here. Her great-grandfather was a Watusi, who are among the tallest people on earth. I'm sure in our country she might be a fashion model but here she has developed an ability to hear birds, the honey guides in particular. Birds are highly revered by all indigenous peoples, including the Bushmen.

Tuliliki told us that in a childhood vision she saw her people in a circle with purple spears, not of wood and stone, but dripping with purple/gold honey. She has stayed true to this vision from her childhood by learning the songs of each of the Honey Guides, which she can both interpret and mimic.

Because Tuliliki has stayed true to her vision, she is respected. For the Bushmen, social standing is not based on wealth but on how generous you are and how true you have been to your childhood vision, your quest. It was becoming clear why I was not laughed at or treated with condescension; instead, I have been taken seriously and assisted in my Quest. It is that the Bushmen have not forgotten the importance of having a quest and of becoming a guardian of something larger than yourself. Tuliliki exemplifies this.

The Sacred Journey to the First Hive Begins

Preparations are being made for our departure; the men are wishing us well and singing our praises while we beat the drum. Uukule and I danced late into the night and had a chance to share what was in our hearts. He was invited to stay with the Great uLangalibalela and Xhabbo on the Plateau. They were going to initiate him as a dreamer. So in a way he would be following me every step of the way. We all fell asleep around the fire. The night was rich with dreams on the threshold of this great adventure.

We set off at dawn. The woman were dressed in white robes, Tuliliki in front setting a brisk pace and calling the songs that the others would respond to. It had the feeling of a procession, a sacred march. I wanted to be a part of more of these moments. All of it was living, even the time in Mt. Albert sitting in a classroom, but certainly this was more vital and intense--and was this not an education? I was following a dream with people who honoured the pursuit of dreams. This seemed to me to be really living.

I can remember parts of the chants.

There is nothing more delicious than the taste of golden honey
There is nothing more beautiful than a drop of liquid sunlight
If you seek the Hive you must walk the path of beauty

> May I walk the path of beauty in a sacred way
> May this sacred way bring sweetness to those I love.

All this was sung in low, tone-like chants and in a call and response fashion. The song was created gradually verse-by-verse. After a while I got the hang of it and sang out,

"May I walk in beauty and speak in truth."

The others replied, "May we walk in beauty and speak in truth."

The plateau lay on the eastern edge of the famed Kalahari Desert. Westward from us lay endless dunes of snaking ridges, each with plumes of sand blowing off the crests, like spray off a wave. We carried our lives in skin pouches and sought the only thing more precious than water: honey. We descended down from the plateau into the dunes.

As we entered the dunes, Tuliliki paused and called out, "May the ever-changing sands of time lead me to the honeycomb of my own heart."

We replied, "May the ever-changing sands of time lead us to the honeycomb of our own hearts."

"May this be so," Tuliliki called out.

"May this be so," we all responded.

In this way we entered the most dangerous part of the Kalahari.

Animals of the Kalahari

We were little specks of life in a near-lifeless place. As we walked, Tuliliki described to Mum and me the main animals that share this desert with us.

"The king of this place is certainly the Kalahari Desert lion, it is more slender than other African lions, but certainly among the largest, with a striking golden mane, the colour of dark honey. We must be very watchful of this lion, as the Kalahari Desert is its hunting grounds. It blends in with its surroundings so perfectly that it materializes out of the sand in front of you." I looked over at my Mum expecting her to become pale and turn around; instead, she seemed relaxed and okay.

"Next," Tuliliki continued, "is the aristocrat of the Kalahari, the gemsbok. There are few more captivating sights than three, five, or ten of these magnificent gemsbok disappearing in single file over the crest of a dune during a Kalahari desert sunset. Their massive, straight horns can grow up to four feet in length and are formidable weapons that have dispatched many an unwary lion or hyena. I have seen a convoy of Land Rovers brought to a halt by a herd of gemsbok. They slammed into the Rovers with their horns, smashed the windows and punctured the tires.

We must be very careful not to anger them.

"To watch a springbok is to watch an animal that is so obviously joyful. They seem to possess an exuberance and gaiety of spirit that is seldom matched in the animal kingdom. They can leap great distances on the run and they tend to move in unison. They also do something called a 'pronk,' which is a standing jump of surprising height. They simply leap many feet into the air for no obvious reason--just delight, it would seem.

"There are of course scorpions and the occasional rattlesnake that should be watched out for and avoided. These we see as good omens that keep our attention in the present."

From time to time, a call-and-response song was begun or a folk song that often praised the animals of the Kalahari.

The Bushmen's Quest for Honey

I asked Tuliliki to describe to me one of their quests for honey.

"Twice a year, we collect the honey. We know the location of many hives but must constantly seek new ones so we don't take from any one hive too much or too often. The hives that we gather honey from are the children of the hive we now seek. Yet each is still a large hive, often inhabiting a cave; hanging within a large tree; or in the cavity of a giant, abandoned termite mound. They can be found in many places. We track the honey badger through the forest until we come across the honey bird. I sing to it with its own song; to do this, I must learn the songs of the fifteen types of honey birds, and then I speak the words of the ancient honey language, which comes from a time when humans could speak to all living things. The words of this language are so old that their meaning has been forgotten. If I speak and sing well, the honey bird will trust us and agree to become our guide. This trust and the protocols that go with it have been established over many thousands of years. Each of us knows the terms of the agreement.

"We then set off following our honey bird, which has now agreed to become our honey guide. The honey badger also knows it's in on a good thing and we will need him later on. Often we need to run for hours to keep our honey guide in sight or within earshot. We eventually follow our honey guides out of the forest and onto the vast plains. Then we watch and listen for a large column of drones escorting the queen to her hive. Either of us--the honey badger or our honey guide--will first spot the column. We keep our distance from the column of drones, as these bees are very protective of their queen."

I had read about the so-called Africanized killer bees that originated in a lab in Brazil and have made their way up into North America. A scientist named Dr. Kerr was genetically modifying the European honeybee and crossing it with the genes from an African honeybee. The two species are genetically dissimilar enough that they will not breed together. But by isolating its defensiveness (threat radius) gene, the scientist believed he could make the European bee more productive. It did produce more honey but it also became more aggressive and more prone to attack by swarming. It was vital that this new genetically modified bee remain in the lab; however, an accident occurred--a student released it. This new hybrid bee was unfortunately able to breed with both African and European bees and so it reproduced and spread up though Central America into North America. No one knows the exact reason for our current crash in bee populations across North America but I read that the introduction of this genetically modified bee could be a factor.

At a distance we follow this great, golden, flowing line of drones to the honey capital, the hive. The honey birds are so quick they can dart in and avoid the bees and then with their beaks penetrate the outer hive and extract small amounts of honey. These birds do not destroy the hive. We humans cannot get close to a big hive like this without getting swarmed. However, the honey badger can move in close to the hive, but is very destructive. Over many thousands of years we have learned how to be more efficient by working co-operatively together.

The honey badger begins to move toward the hive while we maintain our distance. The drones swarm the badger, but it has a very thick hide and dense, tightly woven fur. He keeps steadily moving toward the hive while vast numbers of drones stream out of the hive and attack. The honey badger can now no longer see and must move on instinct; it has only so much time before the drones penetrate its thick fur and hide. Right at the hive opening, the honey badger spins around and backs up. The honey badger eats a special diet that produces within its digestive system a gas that puts the bees to sleep for a short while.

"You're kidding me, right?" I blurted out.

"It's funny, no?" replied Tuliliki, as she broke into a big smile.

We all had a good laugh together.

"There's a boy in my class who has gas like that; I'm sure that's what's putting me to sleep," I said.

"Ray," Mum said.

Of course Tuliliki looked sad for the boy, but not before I first glimpsed a small mischievous smile on her lips.

"What then?" I asked.

"Then we can approach the hive; we reach in and carefully remove five of the many combs of honey that are each as big as my arm. They drip with wild purple and gold honey. There is nothing like the taste of it. It tastes of the flowers, of the earth, and all living things around it. It tastes like sunlight--liquid, golden sunlight. We lay one of these combs on the ground away from the hive for the honey badger and express our thanks. We place one of these combs in a tree nearby for the honey guide, and give our thanks to it. For ourselves we put two or three of the honeycombs, depending on the size of the hive, in our honey baskets. We then return home and celebrate by singing and dancing through the night."

"Will the honey guide or the badger be able to help us find the First Hive?" I asked.

"We would not attempt to put the Queen of Queens to sleep; there would be many more drones, and it will be much better protected, but I will listen for and try to speak with the honey guides once we get to the edge of the dunes."

CHAPTER TEN
THE LOST CITY AND THE GREAT FARINI

The Mystery of the Anchor in the Sand

"After that, we'll search for the Anchor," said Tuliliki.

"Anchor?" I cried out in surprise. "In the middle of the desert?"

"Yes, it's close to a place called Mariental, which is 320 kilometres inland from the Namibian coast. It's one of the mysteries of the Kalahari, but we Bushmen recovered it hundreds of years ago from a great sailing ship that was thrown inland on a huge wave. When the sea receded, it left the ship stranded and its crew dead. Before the sands swallowed the ship, we recovered all the metal from the cannons and from this we made steel arrowheads, which was another mystery to archeologists, as we never went through an Iron Age. The anchor we moved farther inland to its current place. Even though the dunes are constantly moving, we know where to find it only at a certain time of year when we can find its position by the location of the stars. So the place is very secret. There, many years ago, the great uLangalibalela's father buried something under the anchor that might point us to the First Hive."

An anchor, I thought. I remembered a story Fa told me of a Native North American medicine ceremony that he attended.

"Fa mentioned a ceremony he attended that had an anchor as a symbol. Fa told me that it was twenty-four hours long, where they sang, drummed, and took some kind of sacred plant medicine. The elders all

65

had feathers with which they made patterns of visible energy that they could send around the room to those who needed it. Sort of like an invisible game of lacrosse. I was fascinated, but Fa was unusually vague on details; he said that one day I would have the opportunity to experience this. Mum put an end to that conversation, but not before Fa told me about how an anchor had appeared in the large bed of glowing coals just before sunrise. During the ceremony, he had a vision of large tidal wave breaking over the earth. He saw that the First Peoples are the anchor holding the remembrance that we humans are simply part of the circle of all living things. When the tidal wave of our culture breaks and recedes, whatever is to come will be born from this remembrance."

Tuliliki said, "We know of this dream of your fathers. It is one of the stories that uLangalibalela tells each year during the rainy season. We know that by holding fast to our traditional ways we are also serving the future."

"What do you know of my father, Tuliliki?" I asked.

"I have never met your father, but uLangalibalela has. You must ask him."

I hope it doesn't seem uncaring to be more interested in this Quest than finding Fa, but somehow I know that if Fa wanted to be found, he would be. This was turning out to be the very best of treasure hunts. Treasure hunts and Wednesday's Show and Tell were two of the things I liked most about school. What was buried under the sands near the Anchor a long time ago was somehow connected to the mystery of the First Hive. Fa told me that there are so many important secrets to be uncovered in the world because throughout human history there have been Guardians . . . Guardians who were not overwhelmed by their own lives and times, but were primarily concerned with the future of humanity and all living things. These Guardians hid what was most precious for when humanity needed it most and was ready for this knowledge. Well, surely now is the time when this knowledge is needed most, I thought. Surely many of these secrets are for NOW.

We circled on a dune high above the oasis at Mariental so as to not attract any attention. Tuliliki said we were coming close to the Anchor point, but that it would not be visible, as even the biggest sand dunes constantly shift from year to year and cover up and expose as they choose. It is like a slow-motion sea, which makes it impossible to mark a single point. However, under this constant movement of sand, the anchor remains still throughout the centuries. After the sun had set, under a clear moonlit sky, Tuliliki brought out a star chart that was created for this very night of the year, many years ago. It was a large scroll made from the paper-like covering of a beehive. It had the positions of the stars for this very night directly above the Anchor. Tuliliki and others would draw a giant compass in the sand and work out where they needed to move to next be in more exact alignment with the star chart. We would move a mile this way and take a measurement; and then move again half a mile and take another measurement; and then a quarter mile; and so on until just before dawn, when Tuliliki announced that the Anchor was now below us. If we were out by only twenty feet, we would not find it as we had no idea how deep the anchor was buried.

The women dug with large, seedpod-like scoops that they had brought with them for this purpose. Everyone slept under the noon sun and then in the late afternoon began digging again. It was like we were dogs looking for a bone. Does a dog ever wonder, *is this the place I buried it?* Does a squirrel ever forget where it buried its nuts? At what point do you give up on a hole and start to dig elsewhere? Do we sometimes just keep digging deeper and deeper because we can't stand the thought that we've wasted our time on this particular hole, when we should give up and start digging elsewhere? I was wrestling with these questions while the women were digging. Sometimes I returned to digging just to shake the questions and clear my mind. I was starting to grow concerned that we would get to the end of the Christmas holidays before I was able to speak to the Queen of Queens. There were only six days left until we had to board our plane. I talked to Mum while she was working alongside the other women. She felt we were near and suggested that I try to focus on this moment.

The Lost City and the Great Farini

A shout went up, and there at the bottom of the pit shone a dark metal object. The women dug around it until there emerged a beautiful, massive, rust-free Anchor from a great sailing ship. There it was, dug up from beneath a sand dune, hundreds of miles from any shore. It gave you the clear impression that there would be something important hidden here. Tuliliki dug under the Anchor, and tied to it was a box. She opened the box and in it was . . . a book.

"A book!" I cried out and then covered my mouth, as obviously it was an important book to the Bushmen. Tuliliki began burning some aromatic herbs as an offering. Normally I would have enjoyed this ceremony, but I had to know the title of the book. I edged closer and closer to Tuliliki until I could see the title.

The Lost City of the Kalahari by G. A. Farini
Published by New York Scribner and Welford, 1886.

Mum could see my wide eyes as I got a glimpse of the book. She began to move closer and lean in. In the next moment, there were two very surprised-looking faces in the middle of the smudging ceremony.

After the ceremony, I asked Tuliliki about the book.

"The book contains a map to the Lost City of the Kalahari. Our legends and stories tell of a great capital before this land became a desert. This land was once a great lake that was 80,000 square kilometres in size. Makgadikgadi was our name for the lake; it was known to be the largest inland sea in all of Africa. Due to climate change, about 2,500 years ago, the lake began to dry up; the sands moved in and began to bury the city. Fifteen hundred years ago, we abandoned this great city, and its thousands of inhabitants divided themselves into smaller groups and became nomadic again. We learned about climate change and how static human civilizations can cause environmental destruction; and so we returned to our traditional nomadic ways."

Tuliliki continued, "Eventually the dunes had completely covered our ancient city, and although it was very alive in our stories, its location was lost. As recently as 1885, no white person had ever crossed the Great Kalahari, which is the fourth largest desert on the planet. The first white man to attempt this was a very unusual man indeed. His name was simply the *Great Farini*. Our stories tell us he was born in your country, Canada, the land where you can walk on top of water for many months of the year, in a kraal named Port Hope. He crossed the biggest waterfall in the world, bigger than the Victoria Falls, on a small piece of iron string carrying a man on his back. He also crossed this same waterfall covered in a sack and doing somersaults. uLangalibalela has a picture of the Great Farini being shot out of a great gun. There were many other astounding things he did. This was a white man of great daring and magic. Many agreed to travel across the Kalahari with the Great Farini, including uLangalibalela's grandfather.

"Many in Canada know of the Great Farini--stories about him are still told," I interjected.

"I should hope so; he was a great Witch Doctor," replied Tuliliki. "So in the year 1885, the Great uLangalibalela's grandfather, the Great Farini, and many other Bushmen set out across the Kalahari and saw an extraordinary sight. Some of the taller buildings of the Lost City were rising up from the dunes. The buildings in the Lost City were hive-like and spiralled up like the ziggurats of Northern Africa. They were made from clay, straw, and sand and were the same colour as the desert. To see these towers spiral up from the graceful curves of the dunes must have been a hauntingly beautiful sight. This was the only year we know that this city was visible above the dunes. The following year, it was gone again, and with it the location was lost. Why we never created a star chart of its location, I don't know. Perhaps uLangalibalela's grandfather did not want it to be found.

"A year later, in 1886, the Great Farini published his book, and in it was a map to the Lost City. A few years after that, a copy of this book was delivered to uLangalibalela's grandfather by a diamond trader sent by Farini. As you know, this book was placed under the Anchor so it would never be lost or stolen. Very few copies of it exist and even fewer of the maps. The way Farini kept its true location a secret was that all of the distances were from the Anchor, which could only be found with our star chart. So although adventurers have headed into the desert with this map, none have found the Lost City of the Kalahari.

"Why would the Great Farini have made all the distances from the Anchor, rather than somewhere like Mariental or the coast?" I asked.

"Ask yourself that question and you'll understand a measure of Farini's greatness," replied Tuliliki.

"Tuliliki, It's very exciting to be looking for a Lost City and don't think I'm not appreciative of the opportunity to be part of this adventure, but I have only a few days left before the Christmas holidays are over and I must speak to the Queen of Queens."

"We have not forgotten your Quest, Ray. Stories tell of our ancient city being built around a great hive, which was in fact the First Hive. We have always shaped our lives around the honeybee; our fate and theirs are one. This city was built to protect the First Hive, and in exchange, the bees gave us an endless supply of honey. We considered the Queen of Queens to be our queen. This queen and her drones also protected us from the more aggressive tribes to the south. We believe that the bees never left the Lost City. As the sands closed in, they continued to live in the hive under the dunes, using our buildings and creating tunnels to the surface for the queens and the drones to enter and exit."

"Ohhhh, now I understand. Wow." It took me a few moments for this connection to really sink in. "When do we leave to look for the Lost City, now that we have the map?"

"At first light," Tuliliki replied.

Journey to the Lost City

That night, in our tent, I told Mum about the Great Farini and the Lost City. So great was my anticipation that it was hard to sleep. Mum shared with me that she missed Fa.

"This is just the type of adventure that he'd have loved," Mum said. Then she admitted that she was starting to enjoy this adventure herself.

"Wow, Mum," I replied. "I can hardly believe that you're saying this."

When I asked her if I could remind her that she had said this, she replied, "Absolutely NOT!"

We set out for the Lost City and the First Hive as the sun rose from behind the distant dunes. The endless smoothly curving lines carved day from night and turned the blackness into blazing sun. This was a day for chanting as we travelled. We joined again in song and sacred procession, our intent flowing like waves of water across the parched sands.

It was a full day's journey across endless, trackless dunes as we followed the cryptic map, stopping only to sip water from our skins. Tuliliki told us it was a kind of fast to prepare us. We kept the sun to our left, but it seemed that we were zigzagging quite a bit. I could see that Tuliliki, who was normally so even tempered, was growing impatient with the map. Mum put her arm around her and suggested we take a few minutes' break. We were short on water and supplies, and if we didn't find the First Hive soon, we would have to leave the desert and hunt and forage in the surrounding bush. This would mean an end to my Quest.

Small Creatures and Meerkats

Fa was so good on adventures, he seemed to know the pattern of them--not what was going to happen, but rather he seemed to know what to look for or what attitude was required at that moment that would lead to a good result. Right now, I was baffled.

Fa would say, "So often the little things come to our aid--the great forces are too busy holding onto their power. Stories tell us it's the small creatures that come to our aid. Like in Cinderella, it is the mice and the birds that see her plight and assist her in realizing her destiny. This pattern is repeated over and over again in story (and all stories are Quests), so this is a key to successful questing."

I looked around and it was then I noticed two small eyes looking at our procession from a burrow in the sand about twenty yards away. Tuliliki later told me it was a meerkat. It ducked its small head down and so I moved a little closer; when its head came up again, I became still. Then it ducked down, and again I moved forward. When it came back up, I was still. This seemed to make it very curious. It ducked down and we repeated this until I was only a few feet away and looking it straight in the eyes. It was standing erect on its back legs; it had biggish eyes with dark, almond-shaped circles around them, and the cutest face I had seen in Africa. Very quietly, I said what first came to mind: "We're in trouble, little one."

The meerkat cocked its head to the side.

"We're looking for the city under the sand," I continued.

It stayed and looked curious.

"We're looking for the First Hive of bees, the Queen of Queens."

Then I clearly heard, "Wait."

This time I was quite sure it was inside my head, but it was a definite message. So I waited. A few minutes later, up from another hole, twenty feet farther away, popped three of these little meerkats. They started to leap across the sand. I turned to our band of women and shouted, "Follow me!" and ran off so as not to lose sight of the little creatures. They were quick and light and they bounded easily across the sand. I was tired and heavy and sank in with every step. I ran down the dunes, sometime rolling head over heels; and sometimes I jumped from the top and slid to the bottom, then without pausing, I climbed and crawled my way up, gasping for breath at the top, not looking back. This was our chance, I was sure of it. If I didn't give everything now, I knew I would regret it.

Finally, I couldn't take another step. I dropped down on a dune and lay there; it was pitch-black with no moon. I have never seen such stars. It was like I was floating in the heavens right in the centre of the Milky Way. The stars were so close I felt I could reach out and pull them down with my hands.

I fell asleep lying on the dune, something that I was told never to do. The scorpions seek your heat and can find you in the dark. I woke up to some squeaking sounds right beside me and the sound of a shell being cracked. The little meerkats had attacked a scorpion that was a few inches from me. I don't know how much later Mum arrived with the other women. She was so relieved to find me. Mum set up the tent.

I told Mum that I had to talk to Tuliliki but she said that whatever it was could wait until first light. That night, while we were inside the tent, I heard the sound of something small hitting the sides, like the beginning of rain, which was impossible here in the desert. Then I noticed a distant hum that grew louder into an immense buzz. Mum and I sat up. We shouted to each other. Somehow Mum got the idea that it was a vast plague of locusts. "Mum, it's bees!"

"Yes, of course!" she replied. Neither of us had ever heard such a large number.

CHAPTER ELEVEN
ARRIVAL AT THE FIRST HIVE

The Cypress and the Hive Entrance

We were all up at first light. We now saw what had not been visible in the dark: To the west a quarter mile ahead, was an ancient, knurled tree growing at the base of the dunes. It was there in the middle of the sands-- not at an oasis, just a single cypress tree that had survived the many thousands of years since the time when this was a lush valley on the edge of a great lake. Cypress trees are the oldest living beings on earth. Just near the base of the tree, we could see the last of the great swarm of drones disappearing into the sand. We immediately headed toward the tree.

Not far from the base of the tree was a tunnel that was approximately the same diameter as the tree's girth. Mum, Tuliliki and I held hands and stood in a circle around the tree; for us to reach around the tree, two more women had to join us in the circle. Such was the girth of the tree, and similar to this was the diameter of the entrance to the hive. After saying a prayer to the cypress as elder of this place, we went to the edge of the entrance to the hive. The tunnel to the hive was smooth and hard, made from propolis that drones secrete as a sealant to create entrances and exits to their hive. The constant buzz and movement in a hive sets up very strong vibrations, and the propolis acts as a dampener for those vibrations. I had read that there are many medical uses for propolis, such as an antimicrobial and an antitumour agent. Tuliliki told us that every element of the hive has specific, powerful healing properties. The propolis also held the sand back and could be maintained even as the sand shifted.

Tuliliki had never seen a hive entrance anywhere near this size.

"Do you think the Lost City is under here?" I asked.

"It's here," Tululiki said confidently. "The stories tell of many cypress and baobab trees surrounding the capital. That this one has survived is a clear sign, perhaps the bees provide it with sufficient moisture to keep it alive and so it serves as a marker for their entrance."

There was little doubt that this spot had magical properties. There was power to it that I could feel. Partly because of the fact that it was a tree growing in the middle of the desert, but there was much more--perhaps it was the proximity to the First Hive, or the fact that below us in the sands was an ancient city that thousands had lived and died in over many generations, but I had a sense that there was something else, or perhaps it was all of these remarkable things together.

There was no doubt in our minds that we'd arrived at the Hive of Hives, but there was a big problem that somehow we had not thought of before.

"Tuliliki . . . Mum," I asked, "how are we going to communicate with the Queen of Queens?"

I didn't like the idea of jumping down the entrance directly into an immense hive of African bees. I didn't trust the drones, and what's more to the point, it was unlikely that they trusted me.

Tuliliki and Mum didn't have an answer. We'd come all this way and now we were stumped. There was that uncertainty again!

The Yoga Stick

Our water supply was getting very short, so that day, Tuliliki, Mum, and the other women went looking for a nearby oasis, or, a possible entrance to the Lost City and an underground water source. I stayed by the tree. The drones did not come and go during daylight. This must have been a precaution dictated by the Queen of Queens so that others could not follow the bees and find the entrance to the First Hive. So it was quiet and peaceful under the shade of the cypress. Despite this, I was tense and frustrated. We were so close, and yet, it seemed so far!

Mum had begun to teach me yoga, as she had taught classes in Mt. Albert from time to time. I began with the lion pose and then the mouse. It was an easy and fun way to start. Mostly I liked the animal poses, but it seemed a good thing to start with a sun salutation, as I was in the desert. I began with a series of sun salutations, making sure I also paid attention to my breath, inhaling and exhaling at the right moment in the posture. Following that, I went into the tree pose and held it for a minute or so while I again asked the tree for its assistance. Then I went into the cat pose on all fours with my back arched and my head tilted back. This was for the leopard I'd met in the jungle. While I was looking up, I saw a small branch of the cypress that was in the shape of the cat pose. I smiled at the coincidence. I then went into the camel pose, lifting my arms off the ground and leaning back as far as I could so I was looking straight up into the sky. I remembered that there are no coincidences, so I looked again at the small stick-like branch, and it was now shaped in the camel pose. This was no ordinary stick. It was perfectly still, so I went into the tortoise pose, but to do this you are looking down toward the ground. From the ground I turned my head and looked up, and sure enough, the stick was now in the tortoise pose. This was certainly no tree branch. I had heard about them both at school and from Fa. It could be none other than a praying mantis.

This was the being that I had felt as a presence when I first arrived at the tree. The Bushmen have no single god, but the closest they have to this is Praying Mantis. Mantis is the messenger, and so holds the central place in both their mythology and cosmology. Mantis has many aspects and qualities, not the least of which is a trickster.

The Appearance of Mantis

Mantis can turn itself into a loquacious beggar or even a dead hartebeest! In one tale, the hartebeest had been skinned and laboriously cut up by the children who found it, but annoyingly succeeds in putting itself together again and chases the confused and horrified children into their huts for refuge.

To the Kalahari Bushmen of Africa, Mantis was a Bushmen. There are abundant tales that speak of Mantis and his adventures. In many ways, they are similar to the coyote tales of the Plains Indians and the raven tales of the Northwest Indians. Or much like the *Weesakuchak* (or Whiskyjack) stories of the Midwest. In Norse tradition, Mantis would be like Loki; in Trinidad and Jamaica, he would be the spider Anansi. Fa told me many hilarious stories of the trouble Mantis got himself into. These include all the possible ways that human stupidity can get you into trouble. So the more you realize that Mantis represents aspects of yourself, the more you laugh at the stories. At the end of the story Mantis would finally go to sleep and dream a solution to his problem. These are teaching stories that entertain young and old alike.

Primarily, Mantis is the messenger who travels between the Bushmen and the Creator; this is why the Bushmen pray to Mantis--the praying mantis exists between worlds. It is both here in the physical and it is alien, existing on another plane, such as dreamtime. If you look at Mantis's eyes, you will see that many cultures share the same view of what an alien looks like. Mantis is both the ultimate predator and taker and yet it is also their greatest guardian. In Praying Mantis they are both one and the same. The Bushmen emulate this aspect of Mantis, as they are both hunters (although 80 percent of their diet is vegetarian) and guardians. The other quality that Bushmen value is its ability to mimic and camouflage. It can see but not be seen. Its eyesight is remarkable and so is the speed of its reflexes. It can react in half a blink of an eye. It also embodies the quality of stillness. It remains still until it moves with lightning swiftness.

I had no doubt that the Bushmen's Messenger showing up at this most critical moment was no coincidence. Somehow, somewhere, I felt that Fa was laughing and rejoicing, as were the Great uLangalibalela, Xhabbo, and Uukule. It was all these people, and maybe many ancestors before them, who had brought this to be. I was not alone in my Quest.

Certainly at this moment I was not alone. I looked up at Mantis and he was cleaning himself like a cat. He stopped and looked down at me, moving his head from side to side; this gives Mantis very accurate depth perception. Mantis definitely smiled.

"Are you the Messenger?" I asked.

Mantis stood up on its back legs and bowed its head.

I was filled with emotion. Mantis might be able to take my message to the Queen of Queens. So I told Mantis the story I had heard from the bee back at the aviary when my story began. I told Mantis of the genetic engineering of the African and the European bees and that according to Fa they were continuing their genetic experiments to create bees that would pollinate only the genetically modified crops for which they owned the patents. To do this, they would have to find the Queen of Queens, for only she has the genetic code to create a queen bee. And a hive is dependent on its queen for its own reproduction and propagation. If they captured the Queen of Queens, a company could control the propagation of life for its own profit. This is the ultimate strategy of the taker.

Throughout this, Mantis was still in Prayer Pose. I finished my message with the word, "*Namaste*," which means, "The God in me salutes the God in you."

Mantis opened up its dual sets of translucent wings and flew down into the entrance of the First Hive.

There is no other animal or insect better equipped to enter the Hive of Hives, both by stealth and, if necessary, as a worthy adversary to the drones. On Mantis rode my hope.

Entering the Lost City

There was nothing to do but wait. I was grateful for the yoga as I sat under the tree and thought of how different school would be from this. I was almost looking forward to a little less excitement. Soon Mum and Tuliliki and the other women returned. They had not found any water but they had found a possible entrance to the Lost City through a sinkhole that had formed in the sand. This sinkhole appeared to lead down into the Lost City. We moved our camp that evening to a few hundred feet from the sinkhole. That night, we could hear the humming of the bees in the distance and at first light we lowered ourselves into the sinkhole.

Mum and I had flashlights, and Tuliliki and the others had made torches from melting the wax-like propolis into cloth and then lighting the cloth. The buildings were linked together like the honeycomb of a hive, so we could walk under the sand from building to building. Occasionally, the way was blocked by sand, but we could move through what Mum called "catacombs." That was what this city had become. We could see how people lived and what life had been like thousands of years ago. Everything was perfectly preserved in the dry environment of the desert, away from sunlight. Everywhere there was a hum, like a giant air conditioner, or a big factory. It was of course the hive. Somewhere down here was the First Hive. We seemed to be moving closer to it. It came to be so loud that we couldn't hear each other talk. Still we were drawn to continue, like a siren's call.

I wondered why Mum had not grabbed me to turn around. I was hesitant about continuing and so I turned around for Mum--but she was not there; no one was behind me. I must have lost them farther back. I reasoned that I could just meet them back at the sinkhole if I didn't bump into them as I continued on. I was just too curious to turn back now. I had to see the hive. Not long after, I found that the passage I was travelling along was blocked by sand, but there was a bit of space between the top of the sand and the ceiling, so I climbed up and kind of swam on top of the sand with the ceiling of the clay building right above me. After twenty feet or so, the passage widened and the sand diminished.

The First Hive

I climbed down and found myself in a big cavern. That cavern was clearly once a great city carved from sandstone, overtaken and buried by the desert. We had found the lost city that the Great Farini had searched for!

The hum was deafening. I beamed my light around. On the floor of this vast chamber, under the dust, you could just make out a Maltese cross, above which, in the centre of the cavern, hung a gigantic hive with streams of bees flying into it from many directions. Other than the sheer size, what was most unusual was that through the broken ceiling of the cavern descended the roots of a great tree. The dark-red roots wrapped themselves around the hive, giving it strength and the appearance of veins. The sheer numbers of bees made the hive appear to be pulsing. Between the dark-red roots glowed a kind of golden light, as though the honey still retained the light of the sun; or perhaps it was from the heat of the hive, as this cavern was not cool like the other chambers.

The Chase

It was at this moment that I was apparently spotted by a few drones. Evidently the alarm had been sounded. It was only then I realized the extent of the danger I was in. I considered curiosity to be one of my best qualities, but it could sometimes be a liability. I got back into the passage and climbed over the sand and swam through the narrow section and slid back down and ran. I turned to see a wave of drones pouring through the narrow passage. I ran this way and that; it was like a labyrinth or maize down here.

"Help!" I cried out. It just echoed off the walls.

Next thing I knew, Meerkat was right ahead of me. I knew to follow him. We went this way and that, up over dunes and through many archways and windowed arches. Even so, the drones were catching up and were now flying toward me from openings in several directions. Some were beginning to land on me. It wouldn't be long now. Still, I did my best to keep up with the meerkat, who led me up into a circular tunnel made from hard, wax-like propolis. The surface gave my shoes amazing traction and I was able to run up the ever-steepening tunnel. I could see light--it was getting brighter. I gave one last push and flopped up over the top and onto the dunes. I lay there gasping as millions of drones shot skyward above me. The swarm was so large that the sun went dark. They hovered for a moment and then hurtled down toward me.

Death of the Messenger

Just then I looked over at the cypress tree to get a glimpse of it one last time and I saw, flying toward me, Praying Mantis. The swarm was just a few feet away when Praying Mantis stopped above me and hovered with his four large wings outstretched. The swarm hit continuously for what seemed like minutes. Mantis was knocked from the air and attached himself to my hair. He cried out to me: "Your message got through!"

After his wings were gone, he opened up his protective shell and used it as a shield. The swarm now regrouped following the initial attack and was ready to swarm again. At that moment out of the hive entrance flew thousands of large honeybees, all queens, and there in the centre was the largest bee ever. This must be the Queen of Queens. The swarm of drones hovered in the air. I reached up to my head and gently put Mantis into my hand, his wings were gone and his shell was broken. He was still. The meerkat leaped up onto my lap and licked Mantis.

CHAPTER TWELVE
MESSAGE RECEIVED

Meeting the Queen of Queens

The Queen of Queens slowly flew toward me. I could hear a voice in my head say:

"I'm sorry for your loss, Ray. I have a great respect for Mantis. I can't blame the drones, though; you were too close to the hive, and there was no time to communicate your presence throughout the hive. Mantis told me of your Quest and the peril we are facing. I am developing a plan to have seven Central Hives rather than a single one. Each will be a part of a hub that I will travel between, so my location will not be discovered.

"You and my friends the Bushmen have given so much to bring me this warning and Mantis has given of himself completely. Surely he will be reborn. All I have to give to you in return is this." From under her large wing, she dropped into my hand a small, dried honeybee. "In the future, if you are in trouble, set aside your fear and send love to this bumblebee. It will come back to life and will assist you."

Just then I saw my mum come running toward me, with Tuliliki and the other women behind her.

"Do not fear," said the Queen of Queens, "I have told the drones to hold their places."

Mum was mad at me, but mostly relieved that I was safe. She did not even see the Queen of Queens hovering above me even though she was the size of a large hand. I introduced her to the Queen. Mum looked up and saw above us thousands of queens; and then above them, like a large dark cloud, hovered the drones. It was quite a bit for Mum to take in.

Finally Mum bowed her head and said, "I'm honoured to meet you"

"The honour is mine," said the Queen of Queens. "You and your daughter have travelled a great distance on our behalf, and on behalf of this planet. We are indebted to you both. If there are more Rays, then surely there will come a time when harmony is restored and there will be abundance for all. For my friends the Bushmen and their talented honey guide, Tuliliki, we will allow them to enter the Hive of Hives and return with all the honey they can carry."

Farewell

We wished the Queen of Queens goodbye. She dipped in that special way honeybees do and returned to the other Queens hovering above; together they reentered the Hive of Hives. The drones remained above us, as Tuliliki and the other women took their wicker baskets and descended into the hive. Mum and I stayed there, saying a prayer and preparing to bury Mantis.

"How did Mantis do what he did?" I asked Mum.

"It is the love of a parent for her child; some have this love for those outside of their families. Jesus, another Messenger from the Creator, once said: 'Perfect love casts out fear,' and where there is love, fear does not exist."

"Where is Mantis now?" I asked.

"I'm not sure," replied Mum, "but I do know that Mantis' love is still with us. Can you feel it?"

"Yes, I can."

"I can, too," said Mum; "so that love is now in us. It is eternal."

While we prayed and gave thanks to Mantis, Meerkat dug a deep hole next to the cypress tree, and we placed Mantis in it, wrapped in the leaves of his cypress tree.

Tuliliki Completes Her Quest

Soon Tuliliki and the women returned with giant spears of purple-gold honey, and the drones reentered the Hive of Hives. All of us were much more relaxed, not having the drones hovering above us. Each of the women proudly stood around the cypress tree holding onto their great combs of honey. Tuliliki was down on her knees praying and giving thanks to Mantis, the Creator, and all of us, including Xhabbo and uLangalibalela. Tuliliki had completed the Vision she'd had as a child.

The combs of honey were purple gold and as tall and straight as the spears they used for hunting; and in their midst was a great tree.

I felt grateful, too, and followed Tuliliki's example and knelt down on the sand. I lost all self-consciousness and cried out my thanks to Mum and Fa, to Mantis, to Xhabbo, to Tuliliki and the other women, to Uukule and Moses, to Captain Mopani, to the Queens of Queens, and to Giraffe for his gift. There was so much to be grateful for! We celebrated by each of us holding hands, giving thanks together, and eating our fill of honey. I looked over at Mum and gave her a mischievous grin.

Now it was time to return to the plateau and from there begin our journey home. Another of the women led us on the return journey. Tuliliki was traveling along with us but apart from us. She had completed her childhood vision and so it was vital that she immediately begin her next vision quest, for Bushmen find it very difficult to live without a purpose. To support her vision quest she was not eating everyday food or speaking, and from time to time, the women were preparing plant medicines for her to eat along the way. Every once in a while, I caught glimpses of Tuliliki, and it was scary to see: Sometimes she was covered from head to toe in red earth and at other times she was crawling on all fours across the sand, howling and crying out to the Creator. From time to time, the women would reassure me that Tuliliki was okay.

After a day and a half, we passed through the jungle where I had looked in the eyes of the leopard. I spotted a snake wrapped around a branch but passed it by without its seeming to notice me. Near the mouth of the river was a small freshwater pond where we filled our skins with water and had our first good, long drink. Then we all took off our dusty clothes and ran into the pool shouting, dancing, and rejoicing.

The best way to not take water for granted is to spend time in a desert. I will never see water again in the same way (even just simple things like leaving the water running while brushing my teeth). We washed our clothes and then made our way out of the jungle and around the giant wallow, finally arriving at the bottom of the trail that led to the plateau. The sun was just beginning to set. Uukule and Xhabbo were there to greet us.

Returning to uLangalibalela on the Plateau

It was such a joyful reunion that we began to sing and dance right there. But we remembered Tuliliki and we needed to bring her back to be seen by uLangalibalela and looked after by the rest of the woman of the kraal. All the way up the plateau, it seemed like one sunset after another, just like the days in the Rouge Valley with Fa. It was like he was there with us. Up top, everyone was there to greet us with hugs and fruit drinks, even uLangalibalela. He put his arm around me and we turned to look out at the final moments of the sunset. There was a sense of timelessness here. Just as the last of that great burning circle disappeared, I saw a green streak of light flash across the horizon. I looked over at uLangalibalela with wide eyes, had he seen it? He looked back at me with that same mischievous smile that Fa had had when he'd eaten the honey. I gave him the grin back.

Free to Walk the Land

"I won't take much of your time, Ray, as I want you to enjoy the celebration we've prepared for you--a celebration you so richly deserve. In completing your Quest, you have done me a great favour that I will always remember. I am nomadic. This land is for nomads; it cannot support agriculture for long. If we Bushmen are to join the twenty-first century, we must leave this land. But if we choose to remember and be in the dream, then we must return to being nomads again. There is no middle way for us.

"I have for a long time wanted to walk this land as my father did and his father before him, as this is the only way the land truly speaks to us. But instead, I was entrusted with the guardianship of the location of the First Hive by my grandfather, who was part of the journey with the Great Farini. So I learned and used the ancient knowledge of my people to keep its location hidden. I became known as what you call a "witch doctor." Now that the Queen of Queens has been warned and she has a way to remain hidden, I am released from my responsibility and am again free to walk the land and dream the big dream of my ancestors.

"What I have to say to you is simple: never stop walking the land; it belongs to you as you belong to it. The earth awakes at dawn from its slumber through the eyes and ears of all of us, it dreams through all of us, it shows us the way to true co-operation, it feeds us and heals our spirits. The land is both father and mother. I know that you can see this and it is why you have succeeded in your Quest. I will travel with you wherever you go, Ray."

I thanked the Great uLangalibalela and gave him a long hug.

Ray Tells the Story of the Golden Heart of the World

We danced all night. I danced with everyone and had some special dances with Uukule. Later in the night, there were shouts for me to tell a story. The death of Mantis was too fresh in my mind to tell, so I told the story of going into the Lost City and seeing the Golden Heart of the World and then being chased by bees and Meerkat rescuing me. At which point, Meerkat knew he was being talked about and jumped onto my lap. They wanted me to dance being chased by bees. The drummers kept pace with me, and Meerkat and I danced our escape from the bees. Mum and the others joined in, and amidst much laughter, it looked as if we were all being swarmed. It was good to laugh at something that was so scary at the time.

At dawn, Uukule and I walked out to the eastern edge of the plateau to watch the sun rise. I could really hear and feel how the earth wakes to itself at dawn and promised once a week to wake up early and go for a walk at dawn. Uukule and I talked about how our lives had become woven together like rivers and that we would remember each other and perhaps meet again. We returned to the kraal and went to sleep, not waking until noon. Preparations were being made for our return to the kraal at the end of the road, where we would take the bus back to Windhoek. Uukule would be joining us and again be the bus driver's assistant.

Tuliliki's Vision Quest is Rewarded

Before we left, I went over to Tuliliki's hut. She had dark rings around her eyes but she seemed to be herself again.

"Did you have a vision?" I asked.

"Yes," Tuliliki replied.

"May I ask what it was?"

"Certainly. I was going to share it with you and make a request."

"Anything you ask," I said.

"My vision was of a snake wrapped around a straight branch. I could not interpret the meaning of the vision but when I told it to uLangalibalela, he was certain that it was a symbol he had seen in one of the books your Fa had left behind for treating diseases. On the cover, it had a stick with a snake. It was the same symbol as I had in my dream."

I was confused for a moment and then realized what it was. "Yes, I know I know this symbol--it has been the symbol of all Western doctors from Hippocrates onwards. It's called a caduceus. "

"Then I will become a Western witch doctor," said Tuliliki.

"In my country we do not call them witch doctors," I said. "They don't do magic, or perform miracles; we simply call them 'doctors.'"

Then I realized that this was simply not true.

So I told Tuliliki how they were able to operate on babies that were the size of a person's hand and sew up arteries that are no bigger than a thread using microsurgery. This is surely magic; I realized that they did indeed perform miracles every day.

Tuliliki agreed, but she said, "I don't want to be that kind of doctor. I want to be a doctor of dreams."

I thought for a moment. "Yes, there is also a doctor like this: they are called 'psychiatrists.' Fa often talked about a man named Dr. Jung--he was a doctor that combined the traditional ways of the witch doctor or shaman with Western science."

"That is what I'll become, then," said Tuliliki; "a psychiatrist like this Dr. Jung. Will you help me? Can I return to Canada with you?"

"I would love you to, Tuliliki. Let's ask Mum."

When we brought it up with Mum, she was open to the idea and was certainly willing to give it a try. We packed our things and said our goodbyes. We were sad that Xhabbo had decided to stay and would not be joining us, but we were happy for him, as he seemed truly at home. Soon we were heading down from the plateau toward the bus.

Retelling the Death of Mantis

There was another night of dancing, storytelling, and singing when we arrived back at the kraal where the bus would pick us up. All of us rejoiced that the location of the First Hive was safe and that I had completed my Quest. This time I felt ready to tell the story of the drones' attack and Mantis's death. I had not had time to tell this story to Uukule or anyone other than Mum so I didn't know how the Bushmen would react.

At the end of the story, the people of the kraall took dry, red earth and threw it up in the air. The old men smote the ground and the women wailed. The drum beat irregularly like the heart of the world was stopping . . . gradually, a rhythm formed that united all of us, and through dance it gave us an eloquent way to express our grief. I joined in the dance and was so grateful to unashamedly be able to express my feelings, to literally move through my grief. Before dawn, the elders who appeared to be asleep at the edges of the circle beckoned me over and wished to offer their thanks to me. One had carved a beautiful stick for me. He called me, "Little Old One with the Ray of Golden Light."

Now I could smite the ground with the best of them. Each of them was very lovely and funny.

The bus was ready to go at dawn, and the driver and Uukule were there to welcome Tuliliki, Mum, and me aboard. Uukule got permission, and he and I went to the long seat at the back and stretched out and were soon fast asleep. We slept right through to the entrance to the park. We were surprised how easy it was. The guard did a second take when he saw Tuliliki, but she smiled at him and all he said as he stamped our passes was, "One Bushman in, one Bushman out--it all adds up."

Nothing of note happened, except just as were boarding the plane. I was feeling quite sad that Xhabbo was not joining us, even though I was happy for him. When we checked in at the gate, I asked the flight attendant if Captain Mopani was going to be the pilot on our flight. She replied that he was, and an idea came to me.

So I told the attendant, "This is the first time my friend Tuliliki has flown in a plane. I'm sure she'd be more comfortable if she had a chance to meet the pilot first."

I looked over at her and she nodded. Boy, I must have gotten a little gutsier during this adventure.

"I'll see what I can do," said the flight attendant.

CHAPTER THIRTEEN
RETURN TO MT. ALBERT

The Return Flight

Just after early boarding, we got called to the boarding desk and we were escorted onto the plane and up to the cockpit. Captain Mopani remembered Mum and me and gave us a warm greeting. He asked after Xhabbo and we said that he had wanted to stay in the Kalahari. I introduced Tuliliki to the captain.

"The captain's name means 'osprey,'" I told Tuliliki.

"It's a good thing the captain's name doesn't mean 'ostrich,'" shot back Tuliliki.

Tuliliki told us that her name meant 'honey guide.' Captain Mopani then named each of the fifteen Honey Guides, and with each of the names, Tuliliki mimicked a snippet of their song. I could see that Captain Mopani was smitten. Mum and I would have to watch out for Tuliliki. The co-pilot reminded Captain Mopani that they were already slightly behind schedule for departure.

The flight attendant escorted us over to the seats just behind the cockpit. I looked at my ticket and said, "These aren't our seats--ours are farther back." Mum was trying to shush me. The flight attendant said that we had been upgraded to first class. I thought it better not to ask why. It was great to see Tuliliki filled with wonder as we took off and roared into the sky. I was so excited for her that I lost my own fear of takeoff.

One Little Loose End

There was only one thing I was nervous about. Mum thought I had left Meerkat with Uukule on the bus. But while we were in the back of the bus, I gave most of my clothes to Uukule to give back to me when we met again and I put Meerkat in my carry-on suitcase. Otherwise he would have had to be quarantined, and there was no time for that; and I knew the main hold for luggage was not pressurized, so he had to come on board. I told him very clearly that it was a very long flight and if he wanted to come he'd have to be very quiet. He seemed to understand. Really he lasted a long time without making any noise. Then I started to hear squeaks from the luggage rack overhead. Oh, oh! Then there was scratching. Some other first-class passengers called the attendant. I could see that she didn't really want to find out what was in there. So she asked whose luggage was it. Tuliliki said it was hers; but I couldn't let her take the blame for this so I admitted it was mine. Mum was looking over at me and she wasn't smiling.

"It's my bag," I admitted, "It's a meerkat, the cutest little creature I've ever seen."

"Oh, my," the attendant said. "This could really mean trouble."

The attendant went forward to the cockpit, and a few minutes later, Mum and I were called by Captain Mopani over the intercom.

Captain Mopani spoke in a serious tone and told me that transporting animals is a highly restricted activity and that I could be charged with a few things, even poaching. But that he had checked through a friend in a nearby control tower, and meerkats do not carry any known diseases. He was sure my motives were not bad. So the meerkat could stay in the cockpit for the rest of the flight. However, there would be a problem. Canada Customs would spot the meerkat as my bag went through the scanner.

I had not thought this through very well.

Captain Mopani continued, "As flight crew, my hand luggage is not checked. I have decided to take the meerkat through customs for you."

I clapped my hands and did a little jump for joy. Mum looked over at me and I quickly settled down.

Mum asked, "Are you really okay with this?"

"It's not an easy situation," Captain Mopani admitted, "but I can understand her desire not to part with the meerkat."

Mum responded that it was very kind of him.

"Obviously, she cannot do this again," he ended by saying.

We both thanked Captain Mopani and agreed to meet after the flight.

Tuliliki was delighted for me. I could see that Mum was a bit disappointed by my speedy return to deception. *It's not easy being Mum*, I realized. I went to sleep knowing that Meerkat was having a good time with Captain Mopani and the other flight crew in the cockpit.

The End of Christmas Holidays

We arrived back on Sunday, January 4th, which is Fa's birthday. We called "Xhabbo's taxi driver," as we now referred to him, to pick us up and take us to Mt. Albert. Everything went smoothly and we had Meerkat with us as well.

We were welcomed back by the taxi driver, who looked surprised that Xhabbo was not with us.

"Xhabbo stayed in the Kalahari," I announced.

"Well, I like Xhabbo," said the driver, "but I think you've done pretty well in terms of an exchange."

I was going to say that I considered it rude to insinuate that we were trading in people. Somehow I was going to have to get used to the comments and attention aimed at Tuliliki. So I didn't say anything, as I knew he meant no harm and I was treading carefully with Mum right now.

I decided to give Meerkat a proper name. People thought I was calling him a Mere Cat, and it was annoying to explain, and I didn't want Meerkat to get an inferiority complex about his name. He was fitting in so well and enjoying so much of the neighbourhood. Every insect was a new taste experience for him, although he did also eat the veggie cat food I bought for him. I decided to call him Tuk Tuk, which means "Chief," and also it is the Bushman name for Praying Mantis. So each time I called out "Tuk Tuk," I remembered Mantis and Meerkat and what they had both done for me.

The First School Day of the New Year

On the first day of school, I was back in Mrs. MacFiercesome's class, and everybody got one minute to talk about their Christmas holiday. I could have said I went to Africa on a Quest to protect the First Hive, met the Queen of Queens, and quite possibly helped save the world. But I could just hear the groans in advance. Or it crossed my mind that I could have just gotten up and danced the story, or drummed it, but there's just so much emphasis placed on words at school . . . maybe next year I'll change that.

So I said, "I went on a trip to Namibia and met a real Witch Doctor and I brought back a pet meerkat called Tuk tuk that I wasn't supposed to."

People weren't as interested in that as who went to the latest cool concert, but it didn't fall flat, either.

Afterwards, Wendy, a new girl, came up to me and said, "That's really great. I worked at the zoo this last summer and I'd like to hear more about your trip to the Kalahari."

So I made a new friend.

On my favourite day of the week, Wednesday, our Show and Tell day, I brought Tuk Tuk in, and he was a real hit--except for a few girls who thought that he might bite; or perhaps, "carry some rare new African disease."

I still wasn't very popular, but that didn't matter so much. I have a couple of really good friends along with Mum, Tuliliki, and Tuk tuk. Together we're singing, dancing, and storytelling more, even though it looks and sounds pretty weird some nights in our back garden around the fire in Mt. Albert.

Some of Mum's yoga/granola friends are trying to get me to tell stories in various schools around here. I'm now even more interested in issues like the patenting of genetic code. I want to really know what's going on with this jewel of a planet and find out how to make a difference. Finally, I'm going for more walks in the morning and learning about the Oak Ridges Moraine and the ancient glacial reservoir that's right under my own feet. And yes, I do turn off the tap when I'm brushing my teeth.

But I don't think the world has been saved for all time--I think it's something we have to do over and over again. There's a need for a great many Rays of Golden Light and Guardians. By setting out to be these, we will discover our own unique Quest, and in the fulfillment of that Quest, each of us will experience a greater life than we could have ever achieved as a Taker.

The End

© Verity Jenkins
Whitestone, Ontario
May 7, 2022

ABOUT THE AUTHOR

Verity can often be found writing outdoors in a tent where the walls are thin; participating in the great tide of nature, coyotes howling, driving rain, snow storms, great gusts of wind, geese flying northward, even the occasional opossum lumbering on by.

I have chosen to write under my Grandmother's surname, which is Verity, meaning, "a true principle or belief, especially one of fundamental importance." I am one of a long line of seekers of truth and I hope some of these "truths" have resonated with you.

Please join Ray and myself on our other life-affirming adventures.

Other stories in the series:

Ray 2: The Butterfly Bard
Ray 3: Shambhala and the Caregiving Heart of the World

Also consider: *The Ray Adventure Series Omnibus that is available in ebook, pint and a collector's hardcover edition.*

Please go to www.verityjenkins.com to purchase from all major booksellers and to join the Ray Change Agent community.

Ray Origin Story

Ray is the very tip of a mighty spear that pierces time.

Each one of us, whether we know it or not, is the sharpened head of an arrow that has flown through eons. We see this speck of life we inhabit and don't know that encoded within us is the entire journey of the time-traveling projectile that brought us here.

Our culture does not contain the mythology that allows us to inhabit these broader reaches of time. Yet occasionally we catch glimpses of something much older within ourselves.

My brother David Jenkins, is a medical doctor, my father John Jenkins was a surgeon, his father was a priest, his father was a local General Practitioner in Wales and before that a priest. And so on as far back as our family history goes, doctor, priest, doctor, priest. Like turtles all the way down. What accounts for this pattern?

One day it just became obvious. One thousand years ago on my father's side we were the Druids, the doctor/priests of the ancient Celts, and that pattern has remained written into some part of my nature, and each of my ancestors nature, that hides behind free will.

The Druids were not only the doctors and the priests, they were also the storytellers. It was the bardic portion of what was called the "triple gift." It involved nineteen rigorous years of training to develop. They not only knew plant medicine and were the healers, but they also doctored, steered & maintained the Celtic society as Bards.

Is it possible that I, Verity Jenkins, am the very tip of the spear that traveled through time from the ancients to NOW? Is it possible that you are as well?

What am I carrying that has survived such a long journey? I am carrying Ray. She is the daughter I never had. A modern-day Druidic Priestess in training. Ray's desire to heal the world and be a storyteller has ancient roots. Although she's mischievous and playful, her altruistic nature propels her on adventure after adventure. In her own words, "The world will just not stay saved."

Over and over, since the beginning of human history, heroes like Ray have redeemed the world from our darker nature. What keeps Ray and myself heading towards the light is the altruistic quest, the bardic gift, the wisdom of our ancestors and the wonders of nature.

To the Ray in you,

Verity Jenkins
Whitestone, Ontario

Dear Ray Reader, what's next?

You are at the end of Book 1 in this series. Thanks for joining Ray and myself on this journey to save the pollinators. I hope this story was an inspiration to you and you resonated with the messages.

Although the books in the Ray series can be read in any order, the next chronological story is the Butterfly Bard which can be purchased here and has links to all major booksellers.
https://www.verityjenkins.com/bard

To find out more, here's a link to the Ray Change Agent website. It's my hope that you will sign up for the newsletter and become part of the Ray Team.
https://www.verityjenkins.com

On the site you can access a free *StoryAwake* course that helps storytellers in training to be *Change Agents*. By sharing your story and what you care about - you can change the world.
https://www.verityjenkins.com/storytelling

The author has a patron page for those who support the Ray Vision and wish to help other's change the world by telling Better Stories. If you liked these messages and would consider donating, here's the link:
https://www.verityjenkins.com/support-the-vision

If you want to ask me a question or just drop me a note then here's my email address: verity@verityjenkins.com
Anything else can be found here: https://www.verityjenkins.com/

I hope this story has awoken the Ray in you,

Verity Jenkins

Ray 2 - Butterfly Bard Sample

It began in boredom. Mum has gone out or not come back yet. I start to think of Fa again and why he left. It's a puzzle that I've been over a thousand times and I know it leads nowhere. I've watched too much Netflix or texted too many people and not really felt anything much for a while. I start to think summer holidays are slipping away without anything significant happening. Then I get frustrated with people; I say things I don't really mean, just to start feeling again. Then I go into hiding in my room. Mum calls it a funk: "Ray's in a funk again."

Last term in Mrs. MacFiercesome's class we read *Moby Dick* by Herman Melville. In the first sentence it reads,

"It was a dull grey November in my soul."

If it's actually November, that's okay, but when it's the middle of August, you've got yourself a real problem.

Adults don't have funks; they call them "bouts of depression." When Fa was around, I used to remember him saying, "Call me Ishmael," which are the very first words of *Moby Dick,* right before that part about dull grey Novembers in my soul. So I know Fa also had dull grey Novembers in his soul.

Then Mum returned with really bad news. How is it that things usually go from good to great or from bad to worse? Will had called to tell us that my neighbour Becky, out at the cottage on Lake Erie, had passed away. Becky and I didn't stay in touch during the school year. She lived in Buffalo, New York, and I'm out here in Mt. Albert, Ontario. We would just save up all our news until the summer and then talk and talk for days until we were caught up. It turns out she had a rare and aggressive form of cancer.

This wasn't just a funk anymore; officially I was grieving and so had a good reason to lock myself in my room and have meals passed under the door. This was a pretty black one; on a scale of one to ten, it was a one. I had taken to showering in the middle of night so I wouldn't run into anyone in the hallway. Mum would talk to me outside the door, and nothing really sank in, it just seemed to flow by me as though I were not really there. Then I hit the seven-day mark. Some people believe that God created heaven and earth in seven days, and in as much time Christ was able to rise from the dead, surely I could at least leave my room.

Ishmael concludes the first paragraph: "Whenever it's a dull grey November in my soul . . . I account it high time to get to sea as soon as I can."

Now we're landlocked here in Mt. Albert, and that's a fine thing for a young man who's in his twenties, but for a fifteen-year-old who doesn't even have a driver's licence, it's not good advice. Sometimes I wonder why I couldn't light a giant funeral pyre, or dress in black for a year, or weep and wail for days, or even sit cross-legged in the middle of town and throw ashes on myself. Or even better still, sing and dance and cry and laugh and get drunk and tell stories for days on end. Why couldn't I go on a buying spree, or throw myself like Cato on his sword. (I'd settle for the buying spree.) So many of these things are not available to a fifteen-year-old on a limited budget from Mt. Albert, Ontario.

Secretly I wish I could be a little more histrionic, more dramatic. It feels childish to be hiding in my room. Yet underneath I know those other things are not really what I need to do. I know that it takes time and lots of walks in the woods.

Fa and I would go for nature walks all the time and even Mum and I go on the trail just outside of town whenever we both have a free hour or so. When I was only three, Mum discovered there was a deer living just outside of Mt. Albert and she found one of the places where it spent the night. We'd go out there at dusk, walking so quietly, and feed it apples.

So on the seventh day, I did it: I got out of my room. Mum was out, and I headed straight for the wild little nature trail on the edge of town. For at least half an hour, I had to squint because either the sun had moved closer to the earth or my pupils were the size of a dime. I went off the trail that led to a little clearing, where the deer denned. On the edge of the clearing was a row of cedars with a brook meandering alongside. Wildflowers abounded, and bees made a beeline right by me. Usually they at least slowed down and said a buzzy hello. They probably knew I wanted to be(e) ignored. Butterflies flitted between flowers, and the brook gurgled in a most inviting manner. I went and sat on a tree a beaver had cut down. Even the beaver had been busy around here. Everything seemed so alive and active, even the small trout in the brook seemed to be headed somewhere.

I started to look around and saw a dried pod on top of a milkweed plant. Ever since I can remember I've loved milkweed pods. I opened it up and couldn't help but feel a tiny sense of wonder return.

"Look how perfect those seeds inside the pod are," I whispered to myself. A slight breeze blew across my hand and lifted the little parachute like seeds from inside the pod and hundreds of them took to the air. The breeze circled around me, and so did all the seeds. They did a complete circle and then lifted up above the cedars and out of sight. I slipped another pod into my pocket just in case I needed another boost of wonder.

Then I remembered Fa saying over and over again, "Pay attention to what propagates life. Make life happen." On our hikes and at every opportunity, Fa and I would do something that would "make life happen." Even by opening that seed pod, I'd done just that: I'd "helped make life happen." Immediately I began to feel just that bit better.

"When you make life happen for someone or something else, life happens for you," Fa would end up by saying.

It didn't mean much to me back then; I just liked doing those things with Fa. Once, at the end of the hike I was complaining while picking burs off my clothes, and Fa said, "Even now you're moving those seeds around and making life happen."

I've stayed true to that way of thinking even after Fa disappeared. Last year I literally went to where life first happened, to the Queen of Queens in the First Hive in the middle of the Kalahari Desert in Africa. Bees propagate SIXTY percent of the life on this planet! So they're number one when it comes to making life happen.

When I returned from Africa, I lobbied for and helped create a Bee Garden at Mount Albert Public School. I made and handed out over a thousand buttons that said: "Bee on the Side of Life," and "Bee the Answer." I paid attention to what propagates life, and it gave me the best summer holiday so far.

When I think of milkweed, I always think of monarchs, as they will only lay their eggs on the underside of milkweed plants. It was until recently the safest place to lay eggs, as milkweed is poisonous to most animals. Both Becky's and my favourite time of the year was when the monarchs arrived on Walnut Hill near the end of summer.

Becky and I were taking turns sleeping at each other's place. We would wake up each morning and run outside to see if the monarchs had arrived yet. Then one morning, near the end of summer, we ran outside to be greeted by millions of monarchs that had arrived overnight. Each year, the monarchs congregate on the shores of Lake Erie in preparation for the beginning of their great migration to Mexico. The butterflies were slowly opening and closing their wings, which creates a remarkable optical illusion, as the bottoms of the wings are a dusty peach colour, and the top sides are bright orange with black markings. I ran in and brought out a big pair of Fa's binoculars.

One of our favourite things to do was to zoom in on a single branch and see what was happening up close. Each butterfly weighs only half a gram but they cover every square inch of the tree, which causes the branches to sag under their weight. They pack themselves tightly to conserve heat and energy for their odyssey to Mexico. Up close it looks like waterfalls of saffron and sable. Becky and I then changed the focus on the binoculars to make them out of focus and then we zoomed in and zoomed out with the binoculars. It's one of the wildest sights ever. When I showed Fa, he called it a "moving pointillist fantasy." So far, it's the image I want to remember when I breathe my last breath.

With all those butterflies slowly flapping their wings, the tree looked as though it was just about to lift off. Becky and I wandered around outside all day and just marvelled as clouds of orange with black dots rose up and descended into trees that were already dense with monarchs. For one or two days of the year, this riot of colour descends on the little hamlet of Walnut Hill, marking the start of their long journey south to those hidden valleys in the Transvolcanic Mountains of Mexico.

Then, in the early evening, the winds started to pick up, and by six p.m. there were whitecaps and foam blowing off the tops of the waves. Becky and I started to get worried about the monarchs--surely they were too fragile for this storm. We got our windbreakers on and headed down toward the exposed beach. We had to go up around the breakwall as the waves were crashing in along a five-mile stretch known as Long Beach. When we got there, millions of monarchs were clinging to the sand. Many had torn wings. It seemed such a cruel twist of fate that their journey would end before it had really begun. Both Becky and I were struck with a feeling of hopelessness. We sat there dejectedly in the sand; there was no way to stop the wind. In the end, we just held hands and cried.

Becky was wearing one of my buttons: "Bee on the side of life." I looked at it and thought, *what can we do, we're only two girls*. I knew that was wrong. One of my favourite websites is www.girleffect.org - it takes only one girl to make a difference. "There are two of us, Becky!" I said. "We can't save them all, but what if we go back and get our sand buckets and collect as many monarchs as we can."

"What will we do with them then?" Becky asked.

"We'll bring them into my cottage until the storm passes."

Becky's face lit up, and we both returned to the cottage for pails and then headed straight back to Long Beach. We busied ourselves for half an hour gently filling our buckets with monarchs whose wings were still okay. When our buckets were nearly full with hundreds of monarchs, we headed back to the cottage. Carefully we poured the butterflies onto the carpet. Becky was staying with her Grandfather Will, so she went next door and told him what we were doing. He said that's just the sort of thing Margaret, Becky's grandmother, would have done. He joined us for one trip to the beach but that was all he could manage. Becky and I went back and forth, filling the buckets and emptying them into the cottage.

When Mum returned from Port Colbourne later that evening, she'd had a glass of wine, and it was quite a surprise for her to see hundreds of monarchs opening and closing their wings on the carpet and furniture. Mum joined us for a few trips back and forth and then headed to bed.

Becky and I continued making trips back and forth from Long Beach to the cottage well into the night. We kept going until we were both too tired to even make one more trip. We fell fully dressed into our beds upstairs. That night I woke once or twice to the entire cottage shaking in the wind.

Becky and I rose the next morning to be greeted by sunshine, blue sky and puffy white clouds. We opened the trap door from the attic and looked downstairs. The blue and white cottage was now orange and black. The butterflies were airborne and all fired up to cross the lake, they could see that the storm had passed and they could see the lake, but they were being prevented because a wall of sliding glass doors. We climbed down through the living layer of Monarchs and slowly swam across the room to wake Mum up. Then, together, Becky, Mum, and I opened all six of the sliding doors at the same time. The monarchs poured out of the cottage and rose up into the air and then out across the lake in waves of orange. Will was working in his garden next door. He looked over at that moment and dropped his rake. Al and Arlee, our neighbours on the other side, were on their deck for their usual morning coffee. They both could have caught flies in their mouths.

I remembered how satisfying that moment felt. I could feel a smile creeping across my face from the warmth of that moment. That was making life happen; even the memory of it is satisfying. I thought of how like the seeds in the pod that I was holding in my hand, those butterflies were heading out on a great journey, one that would take them down the spine of North America and would take them four generations to complete the round trip back to Lake Erie. Surely, of all things, that is hopeful. Four generations would be born and die before they would return home. It requires a great deal of hope and faith to set out on such an epic adventure. That's being attuned to the bigger picture. I wanted some of that bigger picture, some of that hope. Maybe I'd find it by following the monarchs to Mexico?

Now I know that many people believe that animals and insects operate only out of basic needs and instincts. It's something I studied a lot. Mrs. MacFiercesome, despise her love of animals, which she hides under her thorny exterior, challenges me a lot on this stuff. But I think I might even be winning her over.

It's still debated scientifically whether animals have emotions. But the evidence for their having emotions is becoming overwhelming, kind of like global warming.

Anyone who has a pet will know that pet has primary emotions such as anger, jealousy, fear, desire, respect, and others.

Let me tell you about Alex, an African grey parrot, that has quite a vocabulary. Researchers taught him the shell game. They would hide a nut under a shell, and Alex could point his beak at the shell with the nut under it, and then he'd be given it. Simple, right? Then they started to move the shell around, and still Alex could correctly identify which shell had the nut under it. Then they brought in someone who with sleight of hand could play the shell game and that person tricked Alex. Alex identified the wrong shell, and when they turned it over, there was no nut. What did Alex do? He banged his beak on the table in anger and swept the game off the table with his wing and then used some words that even the researchers did not know he knew.

Here's what clinches it for me. There is a scientist, Dr. Temple Grandin, a professor in the Department of Animal Science at the University of Colorado, who suffers from autism. She has done extensive research into animal behaviour.

On the question of animal consciousness, Dr. Grandin maintains that in some cases she herself does not pass the criteria that many scientists use to determine if animals are conscious. As a society, we agree that people with autism and the many other humans with marginal or non-existent levels of consciousness, including toddlers and those with advanced cases of Alzheimer's, autism, cerebral palsy, Down syndrome, spina bifida, and others all have the right to live and not suffer. Dr. Grandin says that it is best not to consider consciousness as a kind of on/off switch, which is too simplistic, but rather in levels and stages. This seems much more reasonable to me. I think even feelings work this way. You can have primary emotions like anger and desire and then you can have secondary emotions such as love and friendship. Isn't this likely how we evolved, gradually through these stages of consciousness and through maturing levels of emotions? Why should not the living world around us be on such a journey? Certainly they have some profound things to teach us about what it is to be human.

How is a fifteen-year-old girl, nearly sixteen, going to follow a four-thousand-mile butterfly migration to Mexico, with a risk-averse Mum and a Fa that had gone West of West? It was tempting to descend into another funk. Mum would often say that, "Chance favours the mind that's prepared." The greatest Bard of all time stated, "Readiness is all." Mrs. MacFiercesome pointed out one time that, "William," or "Will the Bard," as I call him, "did not say that readiness is most, or a good idea, or helpful, but that 'Readiness is all.'"

I guess that's pretty significant coming from Will the Bard. Fa said, "Most of us want the bigger life, the life of adventure, but we're not willing to invest in making it happen. We see others enjoying the life we want but we don't see the invisible time where they were preparing out of the spotlight." Was this adventure important enough that I was willing to sacrifice to make it happen? Did I honestly desire this wholeheartedly? Yes; the answer was I did. So the only question was how.

I watched the making of *Winged Migration* and fell in love with ultralight aircraft. What was remarkable was that one of Fa's friends, who lived just a few miles from here in Blackstock, Ontario, was a local eco-hero named Will Leashman. Will pioneered the use of ultralights to follow bird migrations; actually Will led a flock of wayward Canada geese all the way down to North Carolina (there was a Hollywood movie made about him). Will trained them to take off with and follow the ultralight as though it were a part of their own flock. If he could follow Canada geese to North Carolina, why not monarchs to Mexico?

I loved our visits to Will's house, as it's made up of seven interconnected round-domed structures. His house is a beehive, and he's not averse to wild, last-minute adventures like Fa...

END OF FIRST CHAPTER OF RAY 2

To find out more and purchase Ray 2 - The Butterfly Bard
Visit: https://www.verityjenkins.com/bard

Please review this book!

Reviews help authors more than you might think. If you enjoyed the Ray stories please consider leaving a review on the website of the bookseller you purchased this book from and also on Goodreads – it would be greatly appreciated by me.

Say Hello!

You can connect with Verity in a number of places. Verity is committed to supporting readers in telling their story and developing an active community of change agents. If you have a story you wish to tell then reach out to: verity@verityjenkins.com & on the website at www.verityjenkins.com to find out more.